Colleen's Confession

Thousand Islands Brides
Book 4

By

Susan G Mathis

Susan G Mathis

smWordWorks,llc
Fiction

COLLEEN'S CONFESSION
by Susan G Mathis
Published by smWordWorks, llc

ISBN: 978-1-7379366-8-8
Copyright © 2021 by Susan G Mathis
Cover design: Vivien Reis
Editor: Donna Schlachter

Available in print and e-book. For more information visit:
www.SusanGMathis.com/fiction

Visit her at www.SusanGMathis.com
sign up for her newsletter and please consider writing an
Amazon review. Thanks!

PRAISE FOR COLLEEN'S CONFESSION

Susan Mathis weaves yet another tender story of love, hope, and dreams. *Colleen's Confession* captured my heart with the transformative power of art woven into both Colleen's passion and the historical aspects of the region. Readers, sit back and take in another inspiring and moving adventure. ~ Jayme H. Mansfield, award-winning historical fiction author and artist

Such a lovely work of artistry, *Colleen's Confession*. Mathis layers artistry into the main character's deepest dreams as well as the vivid descriptions of the Thousand Islands. The reader is treated to the a page-turning story graced with forgiveness. Social pressure, under-valued people, and low-status create a palpable enemy Colleen must navigate as she finds her way to her God-given purpose. *Colleen's Confession* is lovely, rich, and enchanting. ~Angela Breidenbach, bestselling author of the Queen of the Rockies series & professional genealogist

In *Colleen's Confession* accomplished author, Susan Mathis, magically transports us as readers to an island on the St Lawrence River in the year 1914. We are there inside this story full of twists and turns until the very end. Colleennbecomes enduring to us as she tries to face her pain and fears, past and present. All of the characters have been expertly drawn so that we see them as real as our own family: a son or daughter or perhaps a favorite aunt or mentor. This is a story to remember and treasure. ~Carol Heilman author of *Agnes Hopper Shakes Up Sweetbriar*

Delightful is the word that came to mind as I read *Colleen's Confession*. Author Susan Mathis has done it again with another enchanting story of the Thousand Islands, rich with historic detail and a cast of lovable characters. Colleen Sullivan is an orphaned laundry maid with the heart of an artist and deep hurts to bear. Jack, the handsome Austrian groundskeeper, is her hero-in-waiting, who longs to share those burdens and see her free to soar with her artistic talents. Colleen could behold an exciting future if only she could let go of her past, like so many of us today. Fans of inspirational historical romance will love *Colleen's Confession.* Highly recommend! ~Kathleen Rouser, award-winning author of *Rumors and Promises*

Once again Susan has spun a wonderful story of the servant's life in the Gilded Age. She's done her research of the Thousand Islands, and it shows in her well-crafted story. Colleen and Jack's past were carefully constructed from that research. The faith thread flows nicely through the story adding to their happily-ever-after. I look forward to more from this author. ~Award-winning author Cindy Ervin Huff

Susan Mathis takes us on another journey through the Thousand Islands of the St. Lawrence River. The fascinating settings are like another character in her stories. Colleen Sullivan comes as a laundress to

Comfort Island cottage with a hurting heart from a scarred childhood. Jack Weiss, the groundskeeper, is facing an uncertain future. As he tills the surface of Colleen's heart, they both make life-changing discoveries. ~Janet Grunst, author of *A Heart Set Free, A Heart For Freedom, Setting Two Hearts Free*

Author Susan G. Mathis has penned a rich, powerful story of forgiveness and redemption with strong characters you won't soon forget. Evocative description, realistic dialogue, and page-turning tension draw you into early twentieth century life below the stairs on New York's Thousand Islands. I laughed, cried, and sighed as Colleen and Jack navigated difficulties and unfairness with grit and grace. ~Linda Shenton Matchett, best-selling author *Dinah's Dilemma* and *Spies & Sweethearts*

From the opening pages until the conclusion, the author keeps us on the edge of our seat regarding this unfortunate orphan with a great talent waiting to be discovered. ~Donna Schlachter, author of historical fiction

DEDICATION

To the Thousand Islands River Rats, my faithful readers who love the river as much as I do. Thanks for your support in reading my stories, sharing them with others, and writing reviews on Amazon and Barnes&Nobles. You bless me.

To my wonderful son, Sean, who inspires me with your kindness, faithfulness, and adventuresome spirit. You are a gift, a friend, and a precious man.

ACKNOWLEDGMENTS

I hope you enjoy *Colleen's Confession*. If you've read any of my other books, you know that I love introducing history to my readers through fictional stories. I hope this story sparks interest in our amazing past, especially the fascinating past of the marvelous Thousand Islands. The Clark family is real, and so is the amazing Comfort Island cottage, but please note that I took a bit of creative license in bringing this story to life as some of the timing is a little different than recorded.

Thanks to you, my readers, for your faithful support and for staying connected. I love hearing from you. And special thanks ...

To Judy Keeler, my wonderful historical editor, who combs through my manuscripts for accuracy. Because of her, you can trust that my stories are historically correct.

To Tad Clark, author of *Comfort Island: One Family's Generational Journey*, for sharing so many details about the island. It was so much fun incorporating lots of your memories into my story. And to the new owners of Comfort Island, thanks for the informative Facebook blog you shared and for restoring the cottage to its former glory.

To my wonderful editor, Donna Schlachter, for being a great friend and for sharing your talents with me.

To my amazing beta readers Laurie, Barb, Donna, Melinda, and Davalynn, for all your hard work and wise input. And to Jayme, for your insight into painting.

To my husband, Dale, who even while in heaven, inspires my heroes because you will always be my hero.

To my many writer friends who so willingly write endorsements and reviews, encourage me in my writing, and pray for me. There are too many to name here, but you know who you are. Thank you.

And to all my dear friends who have journeyed with me in my writing. Thanks for your emails, social media posts, and especially for your reviews. Most of all, thanks for your friendship.

And to God, from whom all good gifts come. Without You, there would never be a dream or the ability to fulfill that dream. Thank you!

CHAPTER 1

Colleen Sullivan gazed at the rainbow of colors filtering through the bedsheet billowing in the river's breeze. The setting sun's rich yellows, oranges, and reds melded together to produce the prettiest piece of cloth she'd ever seen.

"If only I could paint it one day." She moaned as she pulled the clothespins from the nearby pantaloons and placed it in the laundry basket. She huffed her angst. "Inconceivable."

She shielded her eyes from the source of the sunset's beauty, the enormous yellow orb casting a rippling path upon the St. Lawrence River. She viewed the Comfort Island cottage aglow in the sunset's brilliance, then peeked back at the sheet. It, too, glowed, a yellow puddle trailing down the white cotton fabric.

What a joy if it would be if she could capture such wonder. She had tried her hand at painting in the orphanage, plucking a few hairs from the old mare, Milly, and tying them together on a stick to make a crude paintbrush. She attempted to create her own paints, too, crushing dandelions, blueberries, strawberries, and the like. But the process never really worked, and she finally gave up, settling for hoarding the nubs of pencils the other children discarded and saving every scrap of paper she could to sketch on when no one was looking.

As a child, she happily volunteered for trash duty, for she sometimes found several sheets of barely used paper, especially in the nuns' bins, which she squirreled away. There were few secrets at the institute, so scrounging a few sheets here or there became a challenge of sorts. To create a genuine artist's sketchpad like she'd seen when a man passed through to sketch something he called waif scenes—although none of the children she knew would be

Aunt Gertie slipped a beige sheet of thin paper from her pocket and handed it to her. She took Colleen's hands, crinkling the papers between her palms. "Peter was on that ship. It was to be his last voyage before coming for you."

What?

Colleen's world spun as she absorbed the news. "My *betrothed*? *My* Peter?"

Her auntie released her hand but placed one on her forearm and kept it there. "Yes. Read the telegram."

Colleen sucked in a deep, steadying breath as she unfolded the missive. She trained her eyes on the words. "Peter Byrne, 23, County Down, perished on *The Empress of Ireland*. Stop. Deceased May 29, 1914. Stop."

Unwilling to believe, she pressed her aunt, vain hope melting as quickly as a cube of ice on a sunny July day. "Perhaps it's another Peter Byrne. It's a common name in Ireland."

Aunt Gertie squared her shoulders. "The telegram was from his mother. He's gone, Colleen, and so is the hope of your marriage."

15

Colleen's eyes brimmed with tears and her bottom lip quivered, but her aunt shook her arm, then squeezed her hands. Hard.

"Stop that right now." Aunt Gertie's tone was as harsh as if Colleen had smashed a fine china teacup on a tile floor. Her aunt scanned the area around them as if searching for something, the long shadows of the early evening, dark and foreboding. "Listen to me and obey."

She pulled Colleen close and lowered her voice, almost whispering. More of a hiss, really. "You will tell no one of this betrothal. No one must know, or they will banish you from your position to grieve the loss. It's Victoria's curse—wearing black and being in seclusion for a year. Ridiculous. A grieving widow cannot work. Do you want that? No. You must earn a wage and move on from this tragedy in complete secrecy. Do you understand?"

Colleen pulled back and searched her aunt's face, the woman desperate to make her understand the urgency and importance of her words. She assented. "Yes, ma'am."

Aunt Gertie puffed out a breath that reeked of garlic. "Good. You must add this secret to the other. No one must know."

Colleen stood straighter, plastering on an air of determination that would fool even Mother Superior. "No one will know."

Aunt Gertie patted her arm and snatched the telegram from her hands, almost ripping it as she did. "I will sequester these away for safekeeping. Be about your work, now. It's getting dark."

"I will."

Her aunt departed up the stone pathway toward the Comfort cottage, taking with her the only hope she ever had for her future.

But *they* must never know. No one must.

She took a deep breath and pulled the last pieces of clothing from the line as night descended. Making her way into the laundry house, she prayed her superior, Mrs. Marshall, would leave her be, at least for tonight. She needed to think, to gather her wits about her, and to understand the implications of the news she'd received. Hope had sunk to the bottom of the river that night with her betrothed.

Though she'd never met Peter Byrne, their betrothal was her ticket out of service. Aunt Gertie arranged the match betwixt her friend, Peter's mother. He would become her family. They would create a family. The first proper family she would ever know. Apart from Aunt Gertie, of course.

A single tear slipped down her cheek and she swiped it away, plunking down on the laundry house steps, despondent. She'd worked for more than half of her life, and she was not yet twenty. She turned and peeked into the laundry—stuffy, hot, smothering. Another twenty years of this mundane existence, and she might as well give up here and now.

Dreams dashed—as her dreams always seemed to be. Flitting away just beyond reach, teasing, twisting her into wretched melancholy. Crushing her vision of the future into shards of the past. One she desperately wanted to leave behind.

Just then, two bats alighted from the laundry's roof and taunted her, swooping and circling her head.

She covered her hair with her arms, swatting at the creatures and shrieking to scare them more than they did her. "Get away from me, you horrid devils!"

Like a whirling dervish, she twirled and dodged them, but the bats seemed unaffected by her antics. Instead, they dive bombed her, flying so close their wings skimmed her hair. "Get away."

From the shadows, a dark figure stepped into a moonbeam of light and gently swatted at the bats with an oar. Jack. His voice was quiet, unshaken by the creatures. Deep but gentle. "Off with the both of you."

In the week since she'd arrived on the island, she'd met him just once when he fetched her from Alexandria Bay. But she'd seen him from a distance several times as he worked around the island. Heart-stoppingly handsome. The sort of man you never want to let too close for he would surely break her heart. Or so Liza, her bunkmate at the orphanage, would say.

His onyx-black hair and brows almost masked him in the shadows. Only the whites of his dark eyes and his glistening pearly teeth were clearly visible until he stepped into the full moonlight. He lowered the oar. "Peace, my fair *fraulein*. They are gone."

Colleen shivered away her nervous repulsion of the creatures. "I hate bats. They're hideous."

Jack bowed, setting the oar on the ground. When he straightened, mirth danced in his eyes. He held back a grin, but the cleft in his narrow chin quivered the tiniest bit. "Mr. Jack Weiss, bat slayer, at your service."

Colleen curtsied. "Thank you, kind sir."

~ ~ ~

Jack rumbled a deep chuckle through closed lips. How could he bring peace to this chestnut-haired *fraulein* with her big brown doe eyes—and perhaps find out what really troubled her? "Actually, bats are an asset here on the islands. They keep the bugs at bay."

Fraulein shuddered. "I'd rather face a thousand mosquitoes than one flying rat." She pointed a slim finger toward the inky sky. "But thank you for rescuing me from those two."

Jack kicked a pebble with the toe of his boot. "I fear you have deeper, more troubling concerns this evening."

The *fraulein*'s coffee-brown eyes flashed a depth of fear he hadn't seen since leaving his Austrian homeland to emigrate to America. She swallowed hard, and her eyes narrowed into tiny slits. "Did you eavesdrop on my conversation with Aun ... ah, Cook?"

"No, *Fraulein.*" He waved his palms to clarify. "I didn't even see that Cook visited with you. It's just that I saw..."

"What? What did you see? Or *think* you saw?" Her face was turning as red as the sunset he'd just admired.

The *fraulein*'s defensiveness, the desperation in her voice, warned him to retreat. Fast.

Jack clasped his hands behind his back, ready to leave. Quick. "It was nothing. *Grüss Gott.*"

Fraulein Sullivan grasped his upper arm and held him there. "No. What did you see? Tell me." She squeezed harder, sending a shock wave through his body—and surprise to her eyes. As if stung, she released his arm and stepped back. "Sorry. Please tell me."

"Sadness."

He had no other word for it.

The lovely *fraulein* peeked back at the laundry steps as if trying to envision the scene. Then her shoulders relaxed, almost drooped, and so did her full lips. And her eyes. Everything turned... sad.

But it was more than that. He couldn't quite put his finger on it. He never was very good with emotions. Especially women's.

But he knew she needed a friend.

"No matter. We all have our days." Jack shrugged, shoving his hands in his pockets. "No need to elaborate."

She stared at him as if sizing him up. Like he did before he chopped down a tree. She rolled her hands over and over each other, then her expression grew somber. "Please, sir, say nothing of my feminine lapse. I must maintain my position at all costs."

Colleen dipped her chin. She stopped halfway up to the house and slowly looked around. "'Tis a lovely evening, is it not?"

He followed her gaze. The full moon cast a warm glow over the two-acre island and the large cottage called Comfort. To the northeast, the St. Lawrence River's main shipping channel spread before them. To the west was The Narrows"—a tight and dangerous passage between Wellesley Island and small islands like this one—and to the east stood New York State, America, in which he'd recently found residence.

Jack settled his eyes on Colleen. "It is. I'm glad to share a piece of it with you."

They finished their uphill climb, and upon arriving at the cottage, Colleen gave another little curtsy. "Thank you for rescuing me. And for sharing about your family. I will pray that war never comes to your homeland."

"You're a *fraulein* of faith? That is good."

Colleen pursed her lips and cast an uncommitted half-smile before retreating into the kitchen.

CHAPTER 2

Colleen climbed the narrow servants' staircase leading to the third-floor maids' quarters. Two other rooms and the attics beyond completed this level of the four-story, sixty-five hundred square-foot cottage, or so she'd been told. She chuckled to herself. Some cottage. It was almost as large as the orphanage she'd called home for almost nineteen years.

Here, though, instead of sharing a room with eleven other girls, she had just the one roommate, a willowy girl with thin, ash-blonde hair and a square jaw. Tara seemed nice enough, but she'd come from Chicago with the Clarks. Perhaps she was a spy tasked to keep a sharp eye out on the new help—her.

Antonio locked her in the basement for spilling the jug of milk, she took a piece of charcoal and drew pictures on the cold stone walls.

No, they did not break her. No one would. Not even Mrs. Marshall, though the woman had tried ever since she arrived on Comfort Island. Would she never be free of cruel superiors?

Colleen moaned as she rolled on her back. There'd be no comfort here, not with that crooked-toothed woman watching her every move with her weasel-like beady eyes and puckered scowl.

A quick rap on the door startled her. The door creaked open. The ogre herself. Marshall. Though she demanded to be called *Mrs.* Marshall, Colleen called her simply *Marshall,* leastwise in her head. Ogre was even better.

"I see you finally found your way back to your bed, Missy. Why did you tarry so long?"

Colleen shifted up on an elbow. She willed her voice to sound as if she'd just awakened from a deep sleep and rubbed an eye with her fist for good measure. "Bats were flying wildly around the clothesline, ma'am. I feared they might soil the clean clothes and bedding. It took longer than expected to retrieve the laundry from the line once the varmints finally scattered."

Marshall let out a grumble. "Well, don't let it happen again. Now, to sleep, and don't wake your roommate. At least she worked hard today."

Colleen acquiesced, forcing her words to sound respectful. "Yes, ma'am. Good night."

The woman clicked the door shut, and Colleen held her breath as the footsteps retreated down the steps. She blew out a breath, but Tara giggled.

Tara whispered, "She's quite the drill sergeant, wouldn't you say? And her voice is so deep she sounds like a man. Why, sometimes I'll hear her calling me and think it is Mr. Clark, though he has been dead for three years now."

Colleen laughed quietly. "It appears the woman has taken a liking to you."

"Only more than you." Tara chortled. "She can be a mean one, I'll grant you that. And she has secrets, I'm sure of it. Been under her thumb for two years.

Yesterday, she smacked my hand for placing the soup spoons in the wrong spot. Today, she pushed me aside when I missed a few dead pine needles while sweeping the veranda. It's best to give her a wide berth and stay on her good side."

"And what about Mrs. Clark? I've met her only once while delivering the clean laundry.
Seems the missus fends rather well with her lady's maid by her side."

Tara tittered. "Aye, they're inseparable. Mrs. Lacey dotes over the missus something fierce. With Mrs. Clark being a widow and all, Mrs. Lacey is exceedingly protective. She wouldn't stand for Mrs. Marshall to even look at the missus wrong. I think she'd lay down her life for Mrs. Clark if need be. I believe they're friends. *Real* friends."

Real friends. What would that be like? The only friend she'd ever known was Magdalene, promptly adopted and whisked away just months after they met, never to be seen again. "Good night again."

Tara let out a sleepy sigh. "Sleep well."

Yes, she'd sleep. Her exhausted body would force her.

But well?

Not after receiving such dreadful news today.

Her future dead ahead—smashed on the rocks and sunk to the bottom of the St. Lawrence, along with her betrothed's body.

~ ~ ~

Sunday afternoons almost made life worth living. Colleen seized the whole two hours off to dawdle and draw. Sketchpad and pencil in hand, she headed for a rocky outcropping on the main channel side of the island. A busy day on the river as skiffs and yachts scurried through the narrows. Ducks, geese, and osprey swooped and soared on the gentle breeze. A few cotton-candy clouds danced high in the sky.

A sailboat slowly made its way along the channel, and Colleen put pencil to paper, furiously working to capture the sight. The long, sleek hull, the bulging sails, the finely dressed captain. As it passed, she filled in the background with the Wellesley Island shore beyond, plus birds, clouds, and waves.

"Ruff! Ruff!"

The island's knee-high, tan-and-white mutt jumped through the bushes and planted a wet lick from her chin to her temple. She'd seen the dog around the island, but never this close. And now, a slimy bath?

"Yuck. What's your name, boy?" Colleen swiped her cheek with her shirtsleeve and gave him a scratch behind both ears, making sure the animal couldn't reach her face with its wet tongue again. "Are you out for a romp?"

The dog promptly planted itself beside her on the rock and settled down for a snooze. Just like that. She'd made a friend. Sort of.

Colleen returned to her sketch, shading in the mast and making the clouds darker and more foreboding. Instead of drawing what she actually saw, she heightened the waves, turning them into angry whitecaps. Then she added more dark shading to elicit the sense of a coming storm.

"You are quite an accomplished artist, but is that what you see now?"

Jack bent down and petted the dog without looking at her. He stared at the river, studied her drawing, then gazed back at the scene before them, as if trying to reconcile the two.

"It's art. I can make it anything I want. That's why I like to draw."

She flinched at her defensive tone and bit her bottom lip, snapping closed her sketchbook and shielding it with her forearm. She didn't need a critic hovering over her, condemning her work. She'd had enough of that to last a lifetime.

Jack's brows furrowed and then rose. He tapped her book. "Oh, it's amazing work. Truly. You have a gift. You must meet Mr. Alson when he comes. He's an artist, too."

The painter who created the murals on the walls of the cottage? She hadn't heard. "He's coming?"

Jack grinned. "He is. And you must meet him."

~ ~ ~

Jack's heart raced at the chance to help Colleen find some joy in life. She seemed so melancholy. Meeting the famous Alson Skinner Clark might be just the ticket out of her gloom. Hopefully, he'd be a benefactor who would guide her in her abilities. From what little he'd seen, her skill was quite remarkable.

He cleared his throat and turned his attention to the dog. "I see you've made friends with Champ. He's a great watchdog. Keeps busybodies and trespassers off the island. Captain Thomson, owner of a boat livery in Alex Bay, rents him out for the summer."

Colleen rolled her eyes. "He's rented? Some watchdog. He came right up to me and planted his slimy tongue on my cheek."

Jack held back a laugh and clicked his tongue. "Oh, I'm sure he's seen you from afar and knows you belong here. He's a bright fellow, really. If you let him, he'll be a loyal friend. He follows me around almost all day long."

Colleen shrugged, twirling her pencil and weaving it through her fingers like a baton twirler. "I'm not sure Mar... Mrs. Marshall would be too keen on having a dog around the clean laundry."

Champ stirred and rolled on his back, baring his tummy to be rubbed. Jack complied—and so did

Colleen. When their hands brushed against each other, the lovely *fraulein*'s eyes widened, and she yanked her hand away as if from a fire. She wriggled her fingers before slipping them under her book. Aloof. Closed.

He continued to scratch the mutt. "I've never met a dog who doesn't like his belly rubbed. As a *junge*... a boy... we had several dogs." Again? How he hated when he slipped into his native tongue. "Did you?"

Colleen blanched. "Did I what?"

"Have pets. Animals you loved. A dog. A cat?"

She shook her head, her thick chestnut locks shimmering in the sunlight. Her nose—turned up just a tad—wrinkled when she responded. "Never. Not permitted. Though some..." Her eyes sparked fear again and she straightened her back. "I mean..."

What was she hiding? Afraid of?

"No matter." Jack cleared his throat. "Would you like a tour of the islands one day? I can take you out in a skiff. When you're free."

Perfect brown brows rose and stayed up while she entertained the idea. Then they fell back to their normal spot. "Perhaps. Though Mrs. Marshall keeps a strict eye out for me, and I should have to be accompanied by my roommate or another, for propriety's sake. But I'm confused. You're the groundskeeper, yet you can captain a skiff?"

Ah, safer territory. "I am. Plus the handyman, and sometimes a first mate, when I run to Alexandria Bay for supplies or transport folks back and forth if need be."

Colleen laughed. "A Jack of all trades? That fits."

Was she making fun of him? Calling him names. His face tightened and mouth drooped. Heat warmed his cheeks and ears.

She sucked in a breath. "Pardon. It's just an expression. I meant no ill. Do you have hobbies?"

So, she wasn't teasing. He blew out a breath and shrugged. "Can't draw a stick figure, but I can do a pretty good chirp."

Colleen's mouth dropped open and snapped it shut. "Chirp? Is that Austrian?"

Jack chuckled. "No, I do bird vocalizations. I make the sounds with my hands. Like this."

Taking his fingertips on both hands, he curled them around each other. With his right thumb beside his left, he created a little cave between the palms of his hands. He pressed his two thumbs together to make a tiny slit and curled his lips around his teeth. Then he blew. Slow and steady, he made an owl call. Quick and sharp, a chirp. Long and low, a dove's call. When he finished, Colleen's eyes twinkled. Joy spread across her face like a brilliant Thousand Islands sunrise.

His heart thumped hard. "I have other calls, but that's my trick. And you? Other than being an upcoming famous artist one day?"

Colleen wrinkled her nose again. "Stuff and nonsense. They are nothing. Just doodles."

Jack pressed his lips together before countering her words. "I disagree. May I see your other drawings? Please?"

After a few moments of tense silence, Colleen reluctantly handed over her notebook. Carefully, almost reverently, he turned page after page of skillful artistry. A glorious island sunset, even without color, evoked a sigh from deep within him. A nest of wrens, the creatures so lifelike, he studied them for flaws but couldn't find any. A stand of oak, elm, and pine trees, methodically detailed. A muskrat sunning itself on the beach. Adorable.

He gently closed the book and returned it to her, tapping the cover as she accepted it. "Colleen, do you have any idea how exquisite these are? Mr. Clark would be pleased, I'm sure. He's painted landscapes and cityscapes all over the world. The murals in the cottage? I'm told he and his artist friends spent rainy days—and likely many sunny days—creating them."

Her brow furrowed, and she tipped her head. "The murals are amazing, especially the German village, though it's still unfinished. But why the Oriental motifs? The huge paper parasol over the dining room table and above the beds in the upstairs guest room. The straw matting on the floor. The Oriental girls on the front staircase and in the upstairs hallway."

Jack grinned. "I've been told it's all the rage, ever since Admiral Perry's visit to Japan. And though Austria is most known for its musicians—Mozart, Beethoven, and others—Vienna is full of art. I have spent many hours gazing at the splendor of its rococo and baroque palaces and churches. Days in the art museums. I must confess that I am a poor man with a rich eye."

Colleen's shoulders settled into a relaxed posture, and a sweet, placid smile crossed her full, pink lips. "That would be a dream come true. To see real art."

Jack shifted on the hard rock. "Oh, but you already have. Mr. Clark's work, which is world renown. Do you know that just last year he went down to the Panama Canal and painted a series of masterpieces featuring the construction? Simply to memorialize the canal. He even ventured down into the construction site. I've seen a few of them, and his attention to detail will challenge you to study each rendering for ages and ages. The canal's machinery and innovation dwarfs the tiny people with the most ethereal use of light I've ever seen and a masterful impressionistic hand."

Colleen let out a tiny chuckle. "You are an art connoisseur. How do you know so much?"

Jack let out a gregarious laugh. Champ popped his head up to question him and then plunked it right back down. He scratched the dog's ear to settle him. *"Grossvader…* Grandfather was a painter and sculptor with the Vienna Succession movement, similar to the French Art Nouveau. He worked alongside famous architects and decorated the facades of buildings with his wonderful art. Just before he died, almost three years ago now, he made me promise to come to America to find a better life—far from the rumors of war. And so, I am here."

"Goodness. That's quite a lineage. So, why are you a gardener?" Her tone held no challenge or fault, simply curiosity. "One determined to fight if necessary."

"Can't draw a stick, remember? I have no talent, though I appreciate the allure of art. Besides, I love the outdoors, the fresh air, and this river." He shrugged at his admission, scratching the back of his neck. "And I love both my homeland and my new home. I would fight for either."

"And I love to draw." Colleen opened the sketchbook to the scene she'd been working on. "Thank you for sharing about your family, but I need to finish before Mar… Mrs. Marshall calls me back to work. Excuse me, will you?"

Jack yielded, wishing he could stay forever. "Of course. It was good of you to show me your work."

Colleen's smile outshone the sunny afternoon. "And of you, to compliment it so."

Jack gave a low whistle that brought the dog to his side. "Come, Champ. Let's take a walk."

With a wave and a smile, Colleen returned to her drawing.

Jack paused after just a few steps. "And, by the way, Mr. Clark will be here this weekend."

Colleen's head snapped up. "So soon?"

He winked, leaving her with what he prayed was a nugget of hope.

CHAPTER 3

Colleen pulled back her bedroom curtains and sighed. "A third day of rain? Blathers."

Tara giggled, raising a brow. "Blathers?"

"It's Irish. The nuns..." Colleen groaned. "I mean, I know folks who used the expression a lot."

"Aye. You're from the orphanage." Tara shrugged as she fastened her last button and slipped on her apron. "I've known from the start."

Colleen spun to face the young woman, planting her hands on her hips. Her heart raced, and her cheeks flamed. "How? How did you know?"

Tara's eyes widened, and her mouth dropped open. She snapped her jaw closed and held out her arms as a mother would to a hurting child. Her merciful tone softened the blow. "It's all right, Colleen. None of us care."

"I do." She wasn't a child and didn't need pity. Moreover, she hated that her secret was out. The backs of Colleen's eyelids burned. "Who knows? Tell me now."

Tara pulled her hands back and hugged herself, her tiny eyes flashing hurt. "I... Mrs. Lacey told me. I don't know who else knows. What does it matter?"

"I'll not have any of you pity me or abuse me." Colleen huffed out a breath. "No. I've had enough of that from the priests, the church, the town folk. Most deem orphans as rubbish, and I am not."

Tara pulled Colleen to her, wrapping her arms tightly around her and holding her there. "No. It might be a rotten bit of luck that you didn't have parents to care for you, but you are a precious child of God, Colleen. Never forget that. No matter what others say or call you or do to you, God loves you and made you for a purpose."

Colleen tugged Tara's arms away and stepped back. "He didn't care then. Why would He now?"

Tara shrugged, her palms open toward the heavens. "There's much I don't understand, but He will show you His plan soon enough. Trust Him. There's an Irish blessing Mama used to speak over me. 'May you never forget what is worth remembering, and never remember what is best forgotten'."

Colleen huffed. She'd heard enough useless chatter. She grabbed her apron, tied it around her, and yanked open the door. "Come. We'll be late for breakfast."

They silently descended the servants' staircase, the air thick between them as they entered the dining room. The only remaining two seats were beside Jack. Tara took the one further away, leaving Colleen to sit next to the man who wanted a peek into her sketchbook. And her life.

She would grant him the former, but not the latter.

Else he'd flee the island, back to Europe, just to get away from her.

"*Guten Morgen.* I hear the rain will finally pass by midday." Jack offered a gentle half-smile, as if sensing her sour mood. "Looks like I'll be working in the house again today."

Colleen agreed, placing her napkin in her lap. "I will, too. There are piles of mending. Can't do the wash in the rain."

"I'm touching up the walls. A Jack of all trades, as you said." He grinned as he took a bite of scrambled eggs and swallowed. "I rather like the variety."

"Pish Posh. There's no variety for me. Never has been." She shoveled a forkful of eggs into her mouth, then washed it down with a gulp of her tea. "And never will be."

Tara leaned over. "What's pish posh? Haven't heard that in a dog's age. My gran used to say that."

Colleen shrugged, taking a more genteel sip of her tea. "Nothing."

Jack chuckled. "Your variety is revealed in your art, Miss Sullivan. The diversity and nuances and variations, even in your pencil drawings, have given me much to ponder these past few days."

"Miss Sullivan." Marshall's deep, curt tone stopped forks midair and brought silence to the room. She directed a narrow-eyed scowl at Colleen. "Aren't you done yet? We have work to do."

Colleen's blood surged. She took a deep breath and a last sip of tea. Dabbing her lips, she whispered into her napkin. "The ogre is on the prowl."

Tara blinked at her words. "Aye. Have a—a good day."

Colleen rose and nodded to Tara and then to Jack. "You, too."

Marshall stood, tapping her toe, heaving and puffing, while Colleen hurriedly washed her dish and cup and then joined her.

Her superior rolled her eyes. "'Tis about time. Dawdling doesn't speak well for your prior experience. Just because you're pretty doesn't mean you're capable." She clicked her tongue and burped. "Did they teach you nothing at the asylum?"

How dare she?

Everything in her wanted to respond, but Colleen knew she'd receive comeuppance or maybe even lose her position if she pushed back too hard. She bit her tongue. She'd promised her aunt she'd stay silent.

Colleen swallowed her ire and followed Marshall into the dining room, fist clenched tightly in the folds of her skirt. The woman pointed toward Mrs. Clark's bed chambers. "Mrs. Lacey wants a word. Do as she bids and then return to your mending. I have more important matters to attend to than the likes of you."

With her nose in the air, Marshall left the room, her footsteps tapping on the stairs to the upper chambers. As she waited for the missus's maid, Colleen appraised the room. The breakfast dishes had yet to be cleared from the large dining table. Over the table hung an ornately decorated Japanese paper parasol over seven feet in diameter. Three walls lined with shelves held Japanese prints and other decorations. Beautifully painted murals created a dramatic ambiance.

Such extravagance for a summer cottage.

She huffed as she turned to examine the fourth wall. Two windows let in the morning sunshine that broke through the clouds, sprinkling it on the five folding hand fans encircling a painting, which she suspected Mr. Clark had created. On the wall facing the living room, a mural of ducks in flight graced the wall just below the ceiling.

Enjoying the art dispelled the irritation left by Marshall's overbearing manner and the morning's gloominess. What would it be like to spend every day creating pieces of beauty instead of being chained to the drudgery of laundry service? She'd likely never know.

Mrs. Lacey interrupted her musings as she came through the bedchamber door. "I'm glad you're here, Miss Sullivan. We had a minor accident this morning. The perfume bottle tumbled out of our hands and spilled on the table cover, the vanity bench, the rug. It also splashed on the bedding. It's altogether quite an overwhelming job, but I must accompany Mrs. Clark to the mainland today. She's waiting for me at the boathouse as we speak. Can you clean this up, please? We'd be ever so grateful."

The maid bid her to enter Mrs. Clark's private chambers, and Colleen scrunched up her nose. Now that she mentioned it, the room did reek of the sweet-smelling perfume, though every window was open. "Certainly, Mrs. Lacey. Be glad to help."

The lady's maid beamed a wide smile. "Thank you. And if you need to get fresh air, go through my room." She pointed to the small bedroom adjacent to the master. "There's a door to the outside."

Colleen assented, her eyes burning from the overwhelming scent. "Thank you. I will."

Mrs. Lacey grabbed her umbrella and hurried out the door. "Ta tah. I won't forget your kindness, Miss Sullivan."

Colleen pinched her nose at the smothering smell. While the flowery perfume might be costly and pleasantly fragrant with a dab behind the ears of a fine woman, poured out in such volume made it offensive.

No matter. She had work to do.

She picked up the towels Mrs. Lacey had apparently used to mop up the spilled liquid. Holding her breath, she promptly took them outside and dropped them on the tiny stoop of Mrs. Lacey's doorstep.

Gulping in a breath of fresh air before returning to the room, she peeled off the bed linens and the table cover, picked up the dressing gown and handkerchief that also smelled of the redolence, and then added them to the pile outside. Once she had removed the perfume-soaked debris, the intense smell subsided so she could breathe.

Colleen took a moment to examine the richly paneled bedroom and adjacent bath. Its roller window shades held painted scenes on them, and the lace curtains framed a lovely view of the main channel. Had Mr. Clark painted the shades?

She glanced out the window where the once-heavy rain had turned to sprinkles. Perhaps the sun would come out fully, and she could get everything washed, dried, and ironed before the missus returned.

Jack popped his head through the partially opened door and scowled. "What stinks in here?"

Colleen wrinkled her nose. "It's perfume. The missus and her maid had a mishap. I'm cleaning it up."

"Goodness. Need a hand?" He stepped into the room, drawing the door wide open. He opened both windows wider and pulled up the shades as far as they could go. "Fresh air and sunlight should help."

Colleen explained what had happened and showed him the pile of laundry she needed to do. "It'll take me all day to wash these. Three blankets and a duvet? So much for mending. However will I do it all?"

Jack gathered the enormous pile into his arms, dropping a few of the smaller items. "Grab those and we'll take them all to the laundry. You can get started and I'll deal with the rug. How's that sound?"

Colleen couldn't believe her luck. How kind of him. But beware… men always have ulterior motives. According to Liza.

Truthfully, Colleen knew little about men at all. Liza, however, seemed to know everything about them. They had sent her to the orphanage at age twelve after her father killed his son in a drunken brawl. Prior to that, her father's pub had been Liza's home, a place of too much learning, too much that she'd freely shared with her roommates.

Careful, Colleen. Careful.

~ ~ ~

"I doubt I shall ever enjoy the scent of this perfume again." Jack plopped the pile on the laundry house floor and swiped his hand over his face. "How can something so sweet be so putrid?"

"Too much of one thing can do that. Balance. Moderation. I think we should live by those words." Colleen sorted the laundry into piles. "Thanks for helping. Are you sure it's all right for you to attend to the rug when you should be painting the cottage?"

Jack chuckled. "Mr. Root supervises me from afar, but he will understand once I explain. He's a good man and trusts me to do what's most important at the moment. Lets me have free rein as long as I complete the list he gives me week to week. Unlike Mrs. Marshall."

"You! What are you doing in here, sir?" Mrs. Marshall appeared in the doorframe, back-lit by the morning mist. "And to whom are you referring?"

A small groan slipped from Colleen's lips, and her pretty face turned peaked.

He sucked in a breath, shifting his weight from foot to foot. "No one, ma'am. Just helping Miss Sullivan bring down the laundry."

Mrs. Marshall wrinkled her pointy nose and took a big whiff, reminding him of a neighbor's ugly bloodhound back in Austria. "What's that stench?" She glared at him from head to toe and clicked her tongue. "Get out of here. She can do her own work, not conscript you to do it for her. Lazy girl."

The woman entered the tiny room and waved an arm for Jack to exit. He stepped out but glanced back. Colleen's pretty face turned ashen as her superior swept her hand in a large arc and slapped Colleen's cheek. Hard. "This is your job, not his, you slothful twit. Flaunting your skin-deep beauty to the likes of him will get you dismissed. Get to work."

After Mrs. Marshall turned to leave the room, Colleen rubbed her cheek. Upon seeing him still there, the woman stomped her foot. "What are you still doing here? Get a move on and leave her be. This is none of your concern."

Jack fled up the pathway to the cottage, his mind spinning at the abusive treatment of the pretty *fraulein*. He'd never seen anyone strike a woman. In all his life. He knew Mrs. Marshall was unkind. But this? This went to cruel.

He clenched his jaw, making the small tick next to his right eye twitch relentlessly. He'd seen a farmhand mistreat a goat once, but why would someone strike a sweet soul like Colleen? Mrs. Marshall was jealous of Colleen's beauty. That was all too obvious, and it infuriated him. He couldn't reconcile it, but the longer he tried to, the harder the vein in his neck throbbed.

What should he do?

What *could* he do?

He chewed on the quandary until his jaw ached. By the time he'd finished eradicating most of the perfume smell from the room, the sprinkles had stopped and the sun came out. He took the vanity bench outside, sure the perfume had soaked into the upholstery and needed to be removed. That was beyond his expertise.

Touching up the walls was a better fit, and for most of the day, that's exactly what he did. Meticulously, he puttied and painted every little scratch and crack and nick. While on the second floor, he took a moment to study the half-painted German town, the bottom half left undone. But why?

Finally, the walls looked almost as good as new. The front screen door snapped shut, and women's voices tittered below him. Should he try to speak to Mrs. Clark about the harsh treatment of Colleen? Perhaps she would put a stop to it.

He gathered his paint equipment and descended the front staircase, pretending to dab a bit of paint here and there on the way down. Perchance the Lord would open the door and allow him to discuss his burden.

Mrs. Clark sat in the parlor, shuffling through a handful of envelopes. Her silvery hair glistened in a ray of sunshine streaming in through the window. She put on her spectacles to read a missive.

Jack cleared his throat, pretending to attend to a spot near the front door needing a bit of paint. "Excuse me, missus. Shall I leave?"

Mrs. Clark smiled, shaking her head. "It's fine. Continue." She assessed him for several moments. "Your name?"

"James Weiss, missus. Though everyone calls me Jack."

Mrs. Clark chuckled. "James. John. Jonathan. All go by the name Jack. Why, I know so many Jacks I can't keep them all straight."

Jack grinned. "Well, I... if I may... I'd..."

Just then, Mrs. Marshall stepped into the room. "You're back, Mrs. Clark." She snapped her head toward him, her crooked teeth filling a menacing smirk. "And you? Don't you know that paint fumes are poisonous? Remove yourself at once, sir. I wouldn't want you to give the missus a headache."

Mrs. Lacey appeared with a silver tray for afternoon tea. "Well, hello there. Sir. Ma'am." Her gentle smile and gray eyes welcomed him while Mrs. Marshall glowered.

"I'll be going then."

Jack bowed to the missus and left the room. Too many females in the same place for his comfort.

As he returned the paint supplies to the boathouse, he grumbled his frustration. He almost had the words out. Almost had the chance to make Mrs. Clark aware of the nasty maid's misdeeds.

He changed out of his perfume-infused clothes and sighed. He needed fresh air. Leaving the boathouse, he grabbed a bucket and clippers. He'd do a little gardening. Perhaps near the laundry.

Jack snipped his way through the lilac bushes, clipping and trimming errant branches sticking out along the pathway. By the time he got down to the laundry house, his bucket overflowed with clippings. He dumped them on the firepit pile to burn later and surveyed the work Colleen had done.

Blankets and the duvet cover flapped in the breeze. The smaller things were nowhere to be seen.

He circled around the bedding, hoping to glimpse Colleen. She didn't disappoint.

Just inside the tiny laundry, Colleen ironed with a fury, her back partway to him. He could just make out her pretty profile, shimmering with a sheen of perspiration. A frown evident, she let out a deep sigh, then stopped, swiped her brow, and continued.

Poor thing. She'll wear herself out working as she does.

And in the hot, humid laundry house? Such a *fraulein* should be in a spacious, breezy home with a tiny babe in her arms, not slaving in a prison of muggy misery.

"*Grüss Gott, fraulein.*"

She startled as he stepped toward her. "You shouldn't be here. If Marsh… Mrs. Marshall sees …" A flicker of sadness—or was it fear?—passed through her eyes, and she bit her bottom lip, pulling it in and holding it there. "Please leave."

"Mrs. Marshall is busy with Mrs. Clark. I just saw them in the parlor. How are you faring?"

Although he hovered near, she made no motion to join him. Instead, she placed the iron on the steamer and rubbed her hands as if they hurt.

"Blankets are difficult to wash. And three?" She stretched her back and rotated her neck. "With all this humidity, I fear they won't dry." When Jack put a foot on the first step, she gasped then held her palm out toward him. "Please don't. If she…"

He stepped back, conceding the space. "Not to worry. I have no intention of getting you into hot water with that woman. I saw what she did to you. It is utterly inappropriate to strike a…"

Colleen's eyes narrowed to slits, and she threw up a hand. "Stop. You have no idea what you saw. Furthermore, it is none of your business. Do you think I'm weak and can't take care of myself? That I need a nursemaid to protect me? No one has ever protected me from the likes of her or anyone else. Why would I need it now?"

Her challenge smacked him in the face. Why wouldn't she want his help? Did she encourage such treatment? "I… I only meant…"

"I know what you meant. I…"

"Shhh … Mrs. Marshall is on her way. *Grüß Gott.*"

Jack slid behind the far side of the laundry house and hid there, praying he'd go undetected. Praying he'd not cause Colleen any more harm.

Mrs. Marshall stomped into the laundry, a growl so loud it overshadowed the twitters of the birds. "Have you been neglecting your duties again? The blankets are as wet as if you just hung them. You've had all day, miss. What have you been doing? Carousing with the vermin from Germany? Stay away from that *kraut* or else."

"It's… it's humid, ma'am." Colleen's tone was strong but respectful. "They've been hanging for hours."

Slap! Slap!

"Don't talk back to me. You think you can speak to me like that just because you have a pretty face? If I say you're shirkin', then you are. Now get to work."

Jack covered his mouth to hold back a sharp retort. His blood boiled and surged in his ears. He swallowed the anger raging inside. Colleen was innocent.

He had to do something.

But what?

CHAPTER 4

Before rising from her bed, Colleen rubbed her cheek against the memory of Marshall's blows. They weren't the first, and they'd not be the last, she suspected. She'd been a punching bag for as long as she could remember—for the orphanage workers and the other orphans. How was it that some avoided being a target of cruelty while she seemed to summon it?

"Good morning, Colleen." Tara's cheery greeting rang from the far end of the room. "Sleep well?"

Colleen blinked the sleep from her eyes and sat up, stretching away the night's stiffness. "Yes. You?"

Tara's glimmer came punctuated with a giggle. "It should be a crackin' day. The sky is already blue, and Mrs. Clark is expecting guests for luncheon and board games. Aye, I'm to assist with the party. Mrs. Macintosh and Mrs. O'Leary will come from the mainland. They're Irish names, aren't they? Do you know them?"

Colleen grumbled. "Why do people lump others into one big lot just because they have a similar name or heritage? It's absolutely Byzantine. Naturally, I don't know such women of standing."

Tara gasped. "I'm sorry. I meant no harm."

Colleen softened as she rose to dress. "Me either. Sorry." Cringing at her stinging retort, she undid her braid and combed her fingers through her long, thick hair. "I guess I got up on the wrong side of the bed."

Tara splashed water on her face and dried it with a towel. "I've been told we Irish should stick together and know every other Mick around." She snapped her mouth shut and covered it with her hands. "Oh... I'm sorry. That's what Mrs. Marshall calls us, but I think it might not be nice."

After sweeping her hair into a chignon, Colleen waved a hand. "Others have called me worse, believe me. Truth is, I hate being Irish. The innuendos. The names. The inferences. It's not fair. I've never set foot in Ireland nor have any intention of doing so. I'm an American."

Tara concurred, donning her mobcap. "I'm American, too. My family's from Ireland and I want to visit someday, but I've never experienced prejudice. I'm sorry."

Colleen shrugged off the insult. "No matter. Let's let bygones be bygones."

"Aye, thank you, friend. Truly." Tara opened the door for them to head downstairs. "You're a good person. That's all that matters. An Irish proverb says, 'A light heart lives long.' May you find a lighter heart than you have right now, Colleen."

Colleen tossed her a forgiving smile as they went to breakfast. Even her roommate acknowledged the prejudices of the day. Whom could she trust?

No one. That's who.

At breakfast, Mrs. Lacey led the conversation about the luncheon. "Mrs. Clark is near giddy with excitement at having visitors on the island today. I hope everything is ready. And just think, tomorrow Mr. Alson will be here, and the thrill of having a famous artist in residence will commence."

Her voice rose an octave at the mention of the artist son of Mrs. Clark. She folded her hands in front of her chest and closed her eyes. Was she smitten with the man? Colleen held back an amused chuckle.

Frank, the butler, cleared his throat. Besides opening the door and monitoring civil conversations during the servants' meals, Colleen wasn't sure what else he did. She'd seldom seen him about. His bald pate and wrinkly skin betrayed a man who lived past seventy. Perhaps nearer eighty?

His gravelly voice urged her to sip her tea. "I shall attend to Mr. Alson while in residence. He loves the island, just as his father did, even though Mr. Clark commuted to Chicago often during the summer. If you encounter Mr. Alson, you may address him as such."

Mrs. Lacey dabbed her lips with her napkin. "Remember the grand evenings here on the island when Mr. Clark was alive? Half the river folk attended. They'd laugh and dance until the wee hours. Do you think Mr. Alson would want to carry on the tradition while he's here, and we can again have such parties again?"

Marshall mumbled. "Stuff and nonsense. The cleanup takes days."

The butler snapped a warning glare at Mrs. Marshall before addressing the staff. "If Mr. Alson so desires, we shall see to it and make it a fine affair. Now finish your breakfast and be about your work."

Colleen hid a smirk behind her napkin. Interesting that Marshall irritated even the irascible Frank.

~ ~ ~

By midday, the bedding from yesterday's kerfuffle had finally dried in the warm breeze. A day late, thanks to the dank weather. Colleen ironed out every wrinkle from the duvet cover and even the blankets, though she wasn't sure they needed such attention.

71

She folded and piled them high to carry up the steep path to the back of the house. Along the way, a trio of squirrels chased each other right in front of her, almost causing her to tumble. Thankfully, she saved herself and the bedding, just in the nick of time.

Colleen passed under the screened dining porch as Mrs. Clark and her guests chatted like magpies. Laughing and talking, they sounded so happy that Colleen succumbed to the temptation to catch her breath and listen, just for a moment.

Colleen recognized Mrs. Clark's cheery voice right away. "Yes, Mr. Clark was good friends with George Pullman. They often shared a private railcar on their travels to and from Chicago. And when we came to summer on the island, we often shipped a whole train car of supplies from Chicago, too." Mrs. Clark sighed. "It's different now. I can't believe my husband has been gone these three years already and my boys grew up and are now men out on their own."

A squeaky, mousy voice consoled her. "But Alson will be here tomorrow, dear. He'll bring life back to

Comfort Island with his artistic frame of mind—and deliver much comfort to you."

The three women chuckled, but only for a moment. The mousy woman continued. "But seriously, Mrs. Clark, we are here for you, whenever you want company. I'm sure it's hard being a widow, but know that here on the river you're not alone."

Colleen leaned against the side of the house and sighed. Loneliness had haunted her for as long as she could remember, and the camaraderie of these women pricked her heart. Would she ever know a true, faithful friend?

Another lady with a booming, alto voice interrupted her bleakness. "Remember the theatricals the boys used to perform for us? If I'm not mistaken, they called them, 'The Upper Attic Entertainments'."

Mrs. Clark's gentle laugh accentuated her words. "Indeed, they were. Alson always made the elaborate signage, and Mancel and Edwin had a jolly time making up stories together, practicing for hours before each party. Edwin, of course, played the piano or his banjo at each performance. What dear memories you've brought to the day."

Mousy lady sighed. "They were a highlight of our summers, to be sure. How's Mancel's paint business going?"

"Thriving. Busy all the time."

Mrs. Clark's clipped response caused Colleen to pull away from the wall and right herself. She'd been listening for far too long.

Alto woman boomed, "And Edwin is gaining quite the reputation in the architectural world, yes? I've heard talk of his successes."

Mrs. Clark giggled. "I'm proud of all three of my sons, to be sure. I just hope they keep Comfort cottage in the family for generations to come. Alson paints scenes of it every time he visits, and Edwin loves it here. And with Mancel's penchant for boats, I'm sure he'll want to visit the Thousand Islands often, too."

A tug of her arm threw Colleen off balance, and the laundry tumbled to the ground. She held back a squeal, not sure who was pulling at her or what was happening. Then she caught sight of the ogre, jerking her toward the back of the house, leaving hours of work on the ground.

Mrs. Marshall squeezed Colleen's upper arm so tightly it ached, but she didn't let go. Didn't say a word. The woman fairly dragged Colleen up the back steps and onto the porch before releasing her. She added a hard whack on the arm for good measure before folding her arms over her chest.

Then the woman huffed. She almost growled. Then she hissed. "What in Hades are you doing eavesdropping in on the missus's private conversations? I should have you dismissed right here and now. I should drag you in front of the three of them and make you confess your transgressions and let them deal with you. I should…"

Before Colleen had a second to respond, Marshall grabbed her shoulders and slammed her against the oak door leading to the utility room. Her head hit the hard wood, inducing momentary dizziness. "You will never listen in on private conversations again. Is that understood?"

Colleen bit back tears. She'd not give the ogre an opportunity to see her cry. She squared her shoulders and simply acquiesced.

"What's all this commotion out here?" Aunt Gertie appeared at the adjacent door to the kitchen. She opened the screen door and took in the scene, her horror-struck face turning to fury. "You." She pointed a fat finger at Marshall. "Let her be, or you shall have me to reckon with."

Marshall released her, but not without an extra shove. She turned to Cook and grunted. "This good-for-nothing laundry maid dropped the clean laundry all over the ground and left it there. She's not worth the bed she sleeps in, if you ask me."

With that, Marshall stomped down the steps like a toddler having a tantrum. Colleen adjusted her rumpled clothing, gave her aunt a grateful smile, and glanced out beyond the porch. There, behind the blueberry bushes, Jack stood with his mouth open and eyes flaming.

He'd seen it all.

How humiliating.

Again.

~ ~ ~

Jack had only wanted to kill once, when a coyote attacked his collie, Buddy, leaving his furry friend to die. He was only a lad of eight at the time, yet after he buried his best friend, night after night, he plotted how he would find that evil animal and destroy it.

Those same feelings crept into his heart and mind now.

He'd seen the entire sordid incident. Yes, Colleen shouldn't have been listening to the women. But to be treated in such a fashion?

Barbaric. If only Mr. Root were here to talk to, but he'd broken his leg and was recuperating in his Alexandria Bay home, leaving Jack with the full responsibility of caretaking. How could he take care of this kind of *fraulein*? Colleen needed him, but….

Perhaps Cook would report the situation and solve Colleen's dilemma. That would make sense. Woman to woman. He lifted a prayer for that to happen—and help for him to let it go.

The latter didn't work.

He continued pruning the blueberry bushes, but his festering frustration grew by the minute. Just then, Champ scampered up the pathway, dragging the duvet cover in his teeth.

Why hadn't he picked up the bedding and delivered it safely to the laundry house for Colleen? *Der Dummkopf.* Too busy fuming to think, that's why.

"Bad dog. Let go of that."

Jack dropped the clippers and ran toward the mutt. The dog, however, ran in the opposite direction into the pine-needle covered area still soggy from the week's storm.

Colleen appeared on the porch, and yelled, "Oh, no!" Horror etched her face, her eyes widening as she joined the chase. "Stop, you dumb dog."

Champ scampered into a stand of pines and paused, his tail wagging. He gave the duvet cover a good shake, like he was trying to kill it, and waited for the chase to resume.

It did.

Colleen bolted, holding her skirts well above her ankles. She even outran Jack and caught up to the mutt.

But Champ wasn't ready to give up his prize. The dog held the fabric tight in his teeth and growled as she approached.

Jack joined them, but Colleen oozed with anger. Her eyes. Her face. Everything about her held Champ in contempt. She snapped a warning glare at Jack.

She doesn't want my help?

"I can deal with this situation on my own, thank you very much."

She stepped toward the animal, but he retreated. She lunged for the cloth but slipped on the wet needles and fell face first into the muddy groundcover.

He scowled at the dog who now sat, duvet cover still in his mouth, ears perked in apparent amusement. Jack lifted Colleen to her feet, but a scowl alerted him she was still angry.

"I'm perfectly capable of picking myself off the ground. What are you doing here, anyway? Trying to be my knight in shining armor? Every time I'm in a calamity, you seem to be a part of it. Why is that?" She plucked a leaf from her hair and swiped her face. "I don't need your assistance, sir."

Jack huffed a breath, keeping his voice calm. "On the contrary, miss. Everyone needs a helping hand now and then. I'm not trying to be anything but a friend. I was pruning bushes and came to assist. Period."

By now, Champ had settled to have a snooze, the duvet cover forgotten. Jack grabbed it and handed it to Colleen. "At your service, miss."

He folded his arms over his chest and stood his ground, hoping and praying she'd settle down.

Colleen reminded him of his cousin, Adaline. Independent. Secretive. Prickly. But Adaline had a bad lisp and family, friends, and foes alike teased and taunted her. What made Colleen thus? How he'd like a peek into her past to discover the mystery of this woman.

Ever so slowly, Colleen melted like a block of ice in July. Her shoulders retreated from her ears. Her face thawed. Her countenance weakened. Instead of a hard, angry woman, a forlorn *fraulein* took her place.

"You were simply trying to help. Thank you." She hugged the dirty cloth. "I should get to work and redo all I've done—and more."

The dejection in her voice and on her face evoked a compassion for her he'd seldom felt. "Let me be your friend, Colleen."

Colleen's eyes flashed with fear. She swallowed and tilted her chin high. "Why? Why would you want such a burden? Or are you one of those do-gooders, always looking for something—or somebody—to fix?"

What could he say to tear down that stronghold of self-protection? He'd seen the same in his cousin, and it took years to break through hers. Jack heaved a sigh, shaking his head. "That's not why I want to be your friend. I'm alone on this island, too. I'm a stranger in a strange land. I need a friend."

Colleen surveyed him for a long while. Finally, a slight smile lifted her lips. "Perhaps. But now, I must get to work."

Hope soared, but he held back his excitement. "Maybe we can take a walk this evening?"

Colleen turned toward the pile of laundry. "Perhaps."

Perhaps was a start.

But of what?

~ ~ ~

Jack hung close to the porch, waiting for Colleen to exit after dinner. After rewashing the bedding, she'd come late to the table. He'd finished his meal long before and the sun was setting. Mayhap they wouldn't get a walk in after all.

Several boats passed the island as he pondered what he could say to this hurting soul. She needed to hear words that would build solidarity and rapport without sending her packing. How could he show empathy and goodwill without pricking her defenses?

He was ill-equipped for such a task. Pulling in a thirty-pound muskie, fixing a leaky roof, or yanking out thorny bushes was far easier.

When the screen door squeaked shut, Jack snapped his gaze toward the porch. Colleen stood there, reticent to move. She caught his eye with what seemed a warning.

Keep your distance, sir.

Jack tentatively stepped toward the porch and waved a hand. "Shall we? The sun is setting, and time is waning."

Colleen bit her bottom lip and sucked it in as she descended the stairs. "Just a short stroll. I'm tired."

He kept an arm-width from her as they walked side by side. Thank goodness the walkway was wide enough, made of five-foot pavers. "Would you like to see the boats?"

Colleen dipped her chin. "The only one I've seen is the skiff when you fetched me from Alexandria Bay. Remember?"

He acknowledged their meeting as they rounded the front of the house and descended to the largest of two boathouses. He remembered it well. He pointed to the apartment above. "I stay up there, though Captain Comstock is the primary resident. He takes care of all the Comfort Island boats. He's well known for blowing the *Mamie C*'s steam whistle often."

"What a curious name for a boat." Colleen's furrowed brow questioned him. "Do you know its source?"

"They named the steamer after the Clark's daughter, Mamie, who died when she was just eleven. Before her death, the family vacationed in a place called Old Comfort Point. But because the child died there, they never went back. When they found this island, they dubbed it Comfort Island and the steamer *Mamie C* in her honor."

Colleen placed her hands over her heart and sighed. "How touching… and tragic."

As they entered the boathouse, Captain Comstock looked up from sanding the *Bobby*. "Good evening. And who might this be? I've seen you about but not yet had the privilege of meeting you."

Colleen curtsied, casting him a gentle smile. "Colleen Sullivan, sir."

Captain Comstock had a winsome smile for everyone. His round spectacles gave him an air of wisdom that matched his heart. He patted the boat he worked on. "This is *Bobby*, a fine St. Lawrence Skiff."

Jack ran his hand along its side. "This boat is five feet wide, twenty-four feet long, and several hundred pounds of sailing beauty." He pointed beyond to two more boats. "And over there is the *Buzz,* with its sharp bow and a bronze cutwater. Beyond that, the Clarks' houseboat, the *Balboa*." He turned back to the captain. "Might you have a moment to show her the *Mamie C,* sir?"

"It'd be my pleasure."

Jack gazed at Colleen, her chocolate-fondue eyes melting in a shaft of sunlight dancing on her face. He couldn't tear his gaze from her.

No, Captain. You're wrong.

The pleasure's all mine.

CHAPTER 5

After tossing and turning most of the night, Colleen finally gave up trying to rest, the wee light of dawn now warming the room. She quietly dressed and sought the only counsel she trusted.

Under her aunt's door, a dim light danced amidst the shadows. She listened while grunts, groans, and foot shuffling alerted her that Aunt Gertie readied for the day. She knocked lightly, turned the doorknob, and slowly opened the door. Her aunt put a fat finger to her lips to hush her, motioning her to sit in a hardback chair.

Keeping her voice low, Colleen jumped directly into the reason for her intrusion. "Good morning, Aunt

Gertie." Her gaze bounced from her aunt's face to the door and back again. Everyone should be still asleep, but still... "I need your help." She briefly shared her tales of woe. "What should I do about Mrs. Marshall?"

Her aunt plopped down on her bed, the springs squeaking against her weight. "Do? Stay as far away from that nasty woman as possible, and somehow get on her good side—if she has one."

Well, it's not like she hadn't already tried. And failed. "Any ideas of how I might accomplish that task? You make it sound so easy."

The woman shook her head, her eyes narrowing into puffy pillows. She widened them, then set her jaw, a sure sign her anger stood on a razor's edge. "I don't know how she does it, but Marshall has the missus and her maid completely bamboozled into thinking she's the best thing since Corn Flakes. Even after three years in the Clarks' service, I fear her fiendish power."

Colleen sucked in a breath. Her heart raced, so she placed a steadying hand on her chest. Perspiration tickled her back, even in the morning's cool temperature. "How can that be? What shall I do?"

Aunt Gertie finished buttoning her uniform and slipped on her apron. She shrugged, but her eyes flashed a warning. When she whispered, it was almost a hiss. "As I've cautioned you, Mrs. Marshall doesn't know you're my niece nor that I secured you this position, and she must never know. No one must. For your own safety. And mine. Neither of us can afford to lose their job. Particularly not me. Not at my age."

Colleen rolled her lip over her bottom teeth and bit it, spending several moments pondering the ominous admonishments. "How can I get on her good side if she doesn't have one?"

"Beats me. But you must find a way." Auntie stuck a thick forefinger in the air. "You may be in luck, however. At least for today. Mrs. Lacey said that Mrs. Marshall will be off the island for the entire day, attending to a personal affair. Maybe you can come up with a plan before she returns."

Colleen acceded, her racing heart slowing. "That is good news. And Mr. Alson will be here today. What's he like?"

The woman blinked confusion as she cracked her neck. "Who?"

Colleen winced, but quickly recovered. "Mr. Alson, of course." She plunked her hands on her hips for emphasis. "Everyone talks about him as if he were some sort of celebrity. I've seen his art around the house. He's very talented, but he never finished the German village scene near the bath. Why is that?"

Aunt Gertie clicked her tongue, bending precariously to scratch her ankle. "Blasted mosquitoes." She donned her mobcap and splashed water on her face. "Mr. Alson is indeed a world-famous landscape painter, and a fine man. He's traveled the world and paints like a genius. On walls. On canvas." She patted her face and neck dry, then rehung the towel on the washstand bar. "Can you believe he became a professional artist at nine when his fellow students paid fifty cents apiece for his drawings?" She sucked in a breath and furrowed her brow as if she disclosed too much. She waved an open palm at Colleen. "But Mr. Alson is none of your concern. You must know your place in the scheme of things, and that is one of the lowliest of servants. At least for now. Only a scullery maid is lower than you."

Naturally. 'Twas her lot in life.

Colleen stood and curtsied, giving deference to her aunt, the cook, because, as usual, she was the lowest of the low. She released a tiny moan. "I understand, Auntie."

Her aunt caught her hand. "It won't always be this way. You have a good mind and a solid backbone that should prove assets in the days to come. Just be careful how you use them."

"I will. Good day, Auntie."

She slipped out of the room and hurried outside, blinking back hot tears. The sun barely peeked over the horizon, and breakfast not for another thirty minutes.

A walk might help.

Strolling the perimeter of the island, Colleen mulled over all her aunt had said. The warnings. The baneful helplessness. The admonition to stay far from the artist's presence.

Hope for a better tomorrow abated yet again. Secretly, she wanted to meet this artist son of Mrs. Clark and learn about his profession.

She stopped her meandering and looked up at the wispy clouds speeding past the island. A couple of early morning anglers rowed near the Wellesley Island shoreline. Gulls hovered over the river, dipping down to catch their breakfast of fat fish swimming near the surface. Tiny insects hovered just above the placid water, and once, a fish jumped high in the air to catch its meal.

She etched the picture into her mind's eye. Later she'd sketch it.

"Hello, miss."

Colleen whirled. A man, just a dozen feet from her, fished from the shore behind a rock outcropping she'd just passed.

Who was he?

The man smiled as he reeled in his line and set the pole aside. Thick, dark hair and a well-trimmed mustache accentuated his aristocratic, narrow face. He stepped forward, his dark eyes studying her so

91

thoroughly that she shuddered. Could he be a trespassing hooligan up to some mischief? Should she pick up her skirts and flee?

Champ appeared from behind the rock and scampered to her side, pushing his head against her leg, begging for a scratch. The animal seemed to know the man. Warily, Colleen petted the mutt but kept an eye on the mystery man.

"Alson Clark at your service." He tipped his head and held out his hand as if greeting an equal. "I see you've already made friends with this fine fellow."

Colleen gulped back her surprise and curtsied, forgetting all about his outstretched hand. "Sir. It's good to meet you. But you're up awfully early."

Mr. Alson pulled back his hand, swiped it on his shirt, and grinned. "As are you. Came in on the late train. Jack fetched me near midnight. Couldn't sleep with my insatiable desire to soak in the wonder of this place again. Such scope for the imagination, don't you think?" He paused. "Forgive me. And you are?"

"Colleen Sullivan, sir." Her cheeks warmed, hoping to hide that she was a mere laundry maid. "I work here."

"You?" His words held alarm, astonishment even, as he scrutinized her from her toes to her nose. "I've heard about you."

What had he heard?

She swallowed, shifting from one foot to the other under his penetrating gaze.

After what seemed a lifetime, he relaxed and grinned. Then chuckled. "You're the fellow artist."

Jack. What had he said? He had no right.

"Oh, no, sir. I am not an artist." Colleen waved her hands in the air as if fending off a swarm of hornets. She simply must persuade the man against any false conclusions before he made a mockery of her. "I just draw in my spare moments."

Mr. Alson threw back his head and guffawed. "That's what they all say. Artists are proficient in self-defacement and denial of their rightful creative abilities. I've been told you have exceptional ability.

Inspiration guides your sketches. Your perspective is acute. I want to see your work and decide for myself."

I'll boil him in hot oil. How dare he publicize my private affairs to the likes of Mr. Alson Clark?

Jack will have some explaining to do.

Soon.

~ ~ ~

In the cool of the early morning, Jack happily pulled weeds from the lush flower beds surrounding the cottage. He hummed a Viennese *Schrammelmusik* that his *vater* and his *onkel* had played on the accordion and double-necked guitar when he was a boy. Though the music originated in the immigrant slums of Vienna, the men cared not for its unseemly origin. The Austrian folk songs were lively and happy, incorporating a variety of sounds from other nations.

Jack liked that. If only governments could be so collaborative. Like the ones who were now whispering of war.

His throat thickened at the sweet memories of his childhood. But Austria was changing. He'd read just yesterday of the tensions building within its borders and the growing concerns of war coming to his beloved homeland. He swallowed the homesick thoughts. Today mattered.

And Colleen. He couldn't wait to tell her about his conversation with the famous Alson Skinner Clark.

When Jack caught wind of Mr. Clark's untimely arrival just hours ago, he jumped at the chance to captain the late-night shuttle and pick the artist up in Alexandria Bay, almost begging Captain Comstock to stay warm in his bed while he fetched Mr. Alson. Even in the darkness of the midnight moon.

On their boat trip back to Comfort Island, he had seized the perfect moment. The artist's well-known passion for mentoring young artists opened the door, and the slow-going return trip awarded Jack the chance to proclaim *Fraulein* Colleen's artistic talents, and hopefully, whet Mr. Alson's desire to see her work.

Perhaps Jack could sit next to her at breakfast and tell her all about it. Wouldn't it be grand to have a small part to play in discovering a famous artist? A *woman* artist at that?

The sun rose higher in the eastern sky. The rustle of life breezed through the open, screened windows of the cottage. Staff prepared for the day.

Time for breakfast. And seeing the joy on Colleen's face when he told her the news.

When Jack arrived in the servants' hall, however, something was amiss. As she walked in the door, the pretty *fraulein's* eyes muddied to a stormy brown, glaring at him with disdain bordering on contempt. She whispered something in her roommate's ear, and Tara also cast him a narrow-eyed glare. Both scowled at him as they took seats at the far end of the table and refused to look his way for the entire meal.

What had happened? His confusion made his oatmeal taste like wallpaper paste and his coffee like mud. Appetite gone, he rose and returned to weeding the flower beds nearest the front steps, perplexed by the girls' disdain. For several minutes he muddled it over but couldn't find a reason.

"Has Mother risen yet?" Mr. Alson rounded the path along the nearby lilac bushes with a fishing pole over his shoulder. He held a chain fish stringer holding half a dozen perch. "Would you mind delivering these to Cook? We could have them for luncheon, I suppose."

Jack stood and stretched his back. "I haven't seen Mrs. Clark this morning, sir, but that doesn't mean she's not about." Jack reached for the fish and took them. "Mighty fine catch, I'd say. And so early."

Mr. Alson shrugged. "Had to visit my muse. She's a beauty." He pointed to the river. "I've been all over the world, yet the St. Lawrence and the Thousand Islands are still among the most beautiful places on earth."

"She is. Prettier than the Danube, I think. And the islands, too." Jack glanced out at the river, then surveyed the stringer of fish and held them high. "They are, too."

Mr. Alson plunged his hands in his trouser pockets. "Say, I met your artist friend this morning, but she promptly disappeared when Champ went after my fish. Where might I find her? As you suggested, I'd like to see her work."

Is that what vexed Colleen? What could the gentleman have said to upset her so?

"I saw her a little while ago at breakfast." Jack cringed at the memory of her angry face. "She'll likely be at the laundry house later."

Mr. Alson quirked a furrowed brow. "The laundry? What would she be doing there?"

"Sir, she's the laundry maid."

Goodness. I hadn't told him? She hadn't told him?

If Colleen avoided disclosing such information, what would she say about him revealing her lowly position to Mr. Alson?

The man shrugged. "Hmmm… Better get those fish to Cook while they're still fresh."

Jack snapped a nod. "Certainly, sir. Have a good day."

When he entered the kitchen, Cook assessed him and the catch with a scowl. She grumbled. "Are you dripping fish guts all over my floor? Why are you out fishing at this hour, anyway?"

He shook his head, glancing at the two other kitchen maids who snatched glimpses of him as discreetly as they could. "I'm just the delivery boy, ma'am. These are from Mr. Alson. He thought you could prepare them for luncheon."

"Well, that's different." She motioned for him to bring them to her but turned to the nearest maid. "Tilly, prepare them for luncheon."

The girl yielded and curtsied, but she turned up her nose, displaying her dislike for either the fish or cleaning them, or both.

Jack returned to weeding the flower beds, working his way around to the back of the house, hoping to catch Colleen before she headed to the laundry. He needed to know what bothered her so much.

He stayed at the task for almost a quarter hour, until Colleen finally appeared on the back porch, a basket of laundry on her hip. He sat back on his haunches and waited until she descended the steps before intercepting her.

When she neared, he cleared his throat to announce his presence and not frighten her. "*Guten Morgen, fraulein*. And how are you on this beautiful day?"

Pretending ignorance might be valuable at a time like this.

Colleen's eyes grew wide and stormy. She bit her bottom lip, planted a fist on her hip, and glared at him. "What did you say to Mr. Alson, sir, and when?"

Jack explained the matter as best he could, still unsure why it made her angry. Women were so perplexing. He'd never understand them, but he hoped he'd ease her misunderstanding.

It did not.

Her vitriol oozed out of her very essence as she shifted the basket to her other hip. She almost spit out her frustration. "Well, it's a fine kettle of fish you've put me in. I am not, nor have I ever, claimed to be an artist. I simply sketch for my exclusive enjoyment. I showed you those drawings in confidence, sir. My first mistake. I thought I could trust you. My second."

"I... I only thought..."

She held up a palm to silence him. "Thought? You thought you could divulge my private affairs to the entire world? To present me as something I'm not? To make me out to be a fraud? How dare you!"

Colleen quivered like the Eurasian aspen trees back home, her face the color of a ripe cherry. The *fraulein* had a temper to match his Aunt Liesel's.

Champ galloped to Colleen and jumped up on her, his slobbering tongue ready to soothe her battered soul. But the *fraulein* lost her footing and tumbled to the ground, basket and skirts flying hither and yon. Thankfully, her skirts settled over her limbs, covering her modestly.

Unfortunately, the clothes didn't fare so well.

Colleen blinked, blowing out a breath as she assessed the situation. Champ, unaware he'd done any wrong, continued jumping around her, joy evident in his antics.

She pushed him away. "Get off me, you foul creature."

Champ scampered to Jack's side and nudged him. He rubbed the dog's nose. "It's okay, boy."

Colleen grumbled, rolled onto her hands and knees, and gathered the laundry back into the basket. She brushed off her skirts and adjusted her cockeyed apron, pulling off a few stubborn pine needles. She swept her hair back from her face and picked up the basket.

"May I carry that?"

Colleen held tight to the basket and shook her head vigorously.

Jack had to make her understand. "I'm so sorry, Colleen. I truly meant no harm. I just thought Mr. Alson would appreciate your talents. I know we're all just porcupines in a skiff, trying not to poke one another, yet it seems I've stuck my barbs into you deeply. Forgive me."

Colleen assessed the dog and then at him, her anger deflating like a leaky balloon. Slowly, her eyes softened, then turned… sad.

He liked the anger better.

She licked her trembling lips. "Don't you see? Mr. Alson is a famous artist and will scorn the likes of me. He'll mock my meagre attempts at drawing and dismiss my silly sketches as nothing more than hen scratches. Then I'll become the laughingstock of the island, and he'll forbid me to pick up a pencil to create such nonsense." She paused, her eyes heavy with dejection, before letting out a slow, mournful moan. "Just like always. I cannot abide it."

A vice tightened around Jack's chest, and he heaved a breath. What happened to this fair maiden to cause her to think such things? What had people said about her exquisite creations?

'Twas a deep and dark mystery.

One he must know.

CHAPTER 6

Colleen ironed with a vengeance that turned every piece of clothing she touched into ones with nary a spot or wrinkle. Perspiration trickled down her temples, and she swiped it away with her shirtsleeve, but she didn't stop. Wouldn't stop. She had too much angst to release else she'd burst.

What was she to do? This island was too small to avoid the famous artist for long. No matter how hard she tried to avoid him, she'd surely run into him eventually. Then he'd demand to see her work.

Could she refuse? What if she burned her drawings or threw them in the river, feigning an accident? Perhaps she could hide them and deny they existed.

No. Besides her few personal items, they were the only treasure that was hers alone. The only thing that mattered. That had ever mattered. Others ridiculed and scoffed them in the past. Even confiscated and used them as an example to disparage her in front of the entire orphanage.

She'd never allow such humiliation to happen again.

"There you are, miss." Mr. Alson appeared in the doorway, a cheery wave and smile accompanying him. The mid-day sun back-lit his features, but she knew his voice. He stepped into the small building. "Jack said I could find you here. Do you have a moment?"

Colleen's head spun. She snapped her mouth closed and curtsied. Good thing the bob had become an automatic response to anyone in authority over her.

Did she have a moment? To show him her drawings? Never.

"I'm... I'm working, Mr. Clark. I have duties."

He waved a dismissing hand. "Call me Mr. Alson. Everyone does. I've already talked with Mrs. Lacey. She's your supervisor for the day, yes? She agreed you may take your leave for an hour or two."

An hour or two? Would he take her before the staff and laugh? What else would take an hour—or two?

Colleen swallowed her fears and inclined her head. "Sir, I must finish this pile of ironing before dark."

Mr. Alson chuckled. "My britches can wait a day or two. Come. I want to show you my work. I'm sure you've seen it in your cottage wanderings, but I've a mind to give you a tour—artist to artist."

A whimper escaped her lips. "I'm not an artist, sir. I just draw to relax."

"Do you dream of what you want to sketch? Do they occupy your thoughts and slip into your daydreams while you slave here in this stifling heat?" He wrinkled his nose, his mustache twitching. "Do you love to draw?"

"Always. Always. And always."

Mr. Alson gleamed, his dark eyes twinkling. "Then you have an artist's heart, my dear, so I want to share my work with you." He held out a hand for her. "Will you allow me to present my paintings for your artistic scrutiny? Please?"

Her scrutiny? Was he teasing her? His face showed only benevolence.

She couldn't put him off forever. Best get the derision done.

When she stepped toward him, he waved a deferential hand for her to exit the laundry house first. In silence, they made their way to the Comfort cottage. Since staff only used the back door, she'd never been on the front path or through the front door before, so she paused, taking it all in. The view was indeed grand, a large verandah with a set of staircases on either side, the steps at least six feet wide.

Mr. Alson chuckled. "I've painted this cottage a dozen times or more. Isn't it charming?"

Charming? Extravagant more like it.

"Yes."

He led her up the steps to the double front door with an elaborate brass doorknob—with no keyhole.

Do they not lock the cottage? How unconventional.

Mr. Alson bid Colleen enter first. She stepped into a spacious living room with high ceilings and a set of stairs to the right of the door. But suddenly, she stopped short.

Mrs. Clark and Mrs. Lacey sat in silence, working on needlepoint.

Mrs. Lacey peeped up at her and smiled. "Miss Sullivan."

She beamed a hello to Mr. Alson and then returned to her work.

Mrs. Clark's back was to them, so Colleen wasn't sure how to address her, but Mr. Alson saved her from her quandary. "Mother. Miss. I'm going to show off my work. Want to join us?"

Colleen sucked in a breath.

No. Please. This is awkward enough.

Mrs. Clark giggled without turning to look at her, as if a mere laundry maid getting a tour from him was funny. "I tour it daily, dear boy. Show it off. It deserves fresh eyes."

Did she know?

Mr. Alson chuckled. "Very well." He motioned to Colleen. "Shall we?"

Colleen complied, wishing she could run and shut herself in her room and never reappear.

Mr. Alson waved at a huge painting over the piano. "These two trees still stand by the main channel of the river. I never tire of painting various island scenes. I began lessons when I was eleven and had my first studio in Watertown. Do you know of the town?"

"I'm from there."

Colleen winced. She mustn't disclose such things.

Thankfully, Mr. Alson didn't question her, but with a silent sweep of his arm toward the fireplace, presented a rectangular mural with a similar oval mural on either side. He'd painted a related landscape between two narrow windows and yet another near the front door. All the paintings comprised a coordinating set of bright, cheery trees and flowers in welcoming pastels. Enchanting happy masterpieces.

He didn't comment until they stood in the dining room. "Oriental themes are all the rage, though the fad is waning of late. Still, my artist friends and I spent several summers painting all this. Do you like it?"

Since Colleen had already studied the dining room's art, she gave it a cursory inspection. "It's lovely, sir. I've had the privilege of admiring it recently."

Mr. Alson grinned. "Grand. Have you seen the second floor?"

Colleen shrugged. "Some. The German village…"

"The geishas?"

What are geishas?

She shook her head.

He placed his hand on the small of her back and bid her exit the room. "Come. Let me show you."

Colleen flinched, biting her bottom lip as she passed back through the living room, where Mrs. Clark gave her a quick nod, a twinkle in her eye. Colleen hurried to climb the stairs, but halfway up, the staircase turned, and there on the wall, four larger-than-life paintings of Oriental women in fancy robes greeted her. One stood behind a screen. One had an instrument, and two seemed to perform a dance. Two more lined the upstairs hallway.

Mr. Alson touched her forearm. "These are geishas, performers from Kyoto, Japan. Most geishas receive only the best education and are respected artists and fashion icons, though a few have rather sordid reputations."

Colleen pointed to the mural. "Why the white faces?"

He raised an eyebrow. "I wondered that, too. They paint their faces to reflect the dim candlelight as they sing and dance."

She smiled at the delight of seeing such wonderful art. Of the artist showing her. "They are beautiful, Mr. Alson."

He waved her to continue up the stairs. When they reached the second-floor hallway, he motioned toward the room to the left. "First, the flowers." He opened the door, and a mural of flower baskets greeted them in a cheery tower room. He acknowledged the transom over the door. "I added some flowers there, too, just for fun."

Colleen put a hand to her chest, her heart racing. Such artistry and creativity—on a cottage wall. Her simple sketches would never compare. A small huff slipped from her lips.

Mr. Alson's furrowed brow and down-turned mouth bid her to speak. "You don't like it?"

"Oh, it's wonderful, sir. All of it."

Colleen swallowed hard. How could she find the words to comment further on such craft?

Mr. Alson cast her a tentative smile, letting out a deep breath that settled his shoulders. "You've seen the German village? It's not yet finished, but I rather fancy it." He led her to the mural at the end of the hallway painted partially around the bathroom door. "But I value your honest opinion."

As she had once before, Colleen studied the medieval walled village, a prominent clock tower's hands pointing at five minutes to one. Perfect depth, perspective, shading, and painting. A hint of a moat yet unfinished.

"It's stunning, sir."

He planted a hand high on the bathroom doorjamb, his eyes narrowing. "I'd like you to speak your mind, miss. It's 1914, and I don't give a whit about the master-servant divide that, I hope, is quickly crumbling. I want to hear your thoughts as a person who loves art. After all, it wasn't but a decade ago that a successful Chicago art exhibition gave me acceptance enough to afford several years of European and Canadian travels. Before that, most in the art world considered me an amateur, an unknown. Who knows what the future might bring you?"

Incredulity bubbled up inside of her, and Colleen covered an uncontrollable giggle that continued for several embarrassing moments. Ridiculous. Not her. Never.

"You think that funny? Unattainable? Then let me see your work, and I shall be able to better assess if I speak amiss or not. At the moment, your talents are just hearsay." Mr. Alson folded his hands over his chest as if to challenge her. "I'll be kind, I promise you."

Colleen bit her lip at the request. Dare she? He seemed a pleasant enough fellow.

But could she trust him?

~ ~ ~

The sun hung low over the river as Jack raced down the back steps and along the pathway to catch up with Colleen. "May I walk with you, please? I'd like to show you something."

Colleen's eyes flashed with anger, but then instantly softened. "You may. I wanted to speak with you, anyway."

Had she forgiven him? Oh, may it be so.

They walked along the path toward the laundry house, but he veered them toward the pump house. Shaped like a windmill with a tall tower, its fourteen-foot-square base made it an imposing structure. Its steep-pitched, cedar-shake roof trimmed in Victorian gingerbread that looked like teardrops. Like all the buildings on the island. Along the roof, an intricately spindled railing wove around the structure.

Jack grinned as Colleen stared up at it, her mouth agape. "The windmill powers the water to run uphill where a gravity-fed tank services the cottage—and the laundry. Let's go atop and enjoy the view."

She blinked and squeaked out a gasp. "I couldn't. It's so high."

Jack presented his elbow, his tone more pleading than he wished. "It's worth the climb. You can see for miles."

After several heartbeats, Colleen relented, and they climbed to the top. Her face glowed yellow, then orange, then red as the sun slipped beneath the western horizon. She held tight to the railing, but gazed in every direction before speaking. "Breathtaking. The world is so... grand. Inspiring. Overwhelming."

"It is." He surveyed the scene before them. "Did you know that Mr. Alson builds box kites to take aerial photographs? I've seen photographs. They look like this, only in black and white."

Jack scooted so close that their arms touched. A wave of warmth surged straight into his heart. He darted a quick peek at her pretty profile, and his heart skipped a beat. Or two.

No wonder that beastly Marshall was jealous.

But still. He wasn't worthy of such a talented, beautiful—hurting—woman.

He viewed the Comfort Island beach a few hundred paces away. "Shall we descend before it gets dark and walk the shore?"

Colleen gazed in the distance before responding. "Let's. Firmer ground sounds good."

It was but a minute's walk to the small, sandy beach at the foot of the island. He pointed to the granite ledge in the water. "That's called 'Toothbrush Rock.' It holds back the strong, dangerous river currents and provides a safe swimming spot."

Colleen pointed to a pile of sparkly black rocks on the shore. "What's that?"

Jack shrugged. "Black shale from the spent coal used by the steamers, the house furnace, and the stove. Shall we sit awhile? I need a friend's listening ear."

Colleen agreed, settling on a nearby rock outcropping. "May I go first, please?"

Jack consented.

For several moments, she said nothing. She simply stared at him until his face burned like he'd

shaved too close with a sharp razor. Finally, she broke
the silence. "Mr. Alson showed me his art today and
wants to see my drawings." Her bottom lip quivered,
and even in the growing twilight he recognized
wetness rimming her fondue eyes. "Though you like
my work, I fear he'll find them silly schoolgirl hen
scratches and laugh at me."

Jack touched the back of her hand and stroked it.
Just once. "You've forgiven me, then?"

She acceded but didn't look at him, pulling away
and folding her hands together.

"Colleen, your work is wonderful. I don't know
why you question your talent or doubt yourself so, but
I pray that will change. I've been to the finest
museums in Austria. My grandfather was an artist. I
should know artistry when I see it."

Had he said too much? Too little? He was never
sure.

Finally, Colleen sighed, and a tiny smile crossed
her lips. She readjusted her skirts to better cover her
ankles. "That means a lot. Thank you, Jack. Still, I'm

quite nervous about showing a famous painter my paltry sketches."

Jack shook his head. "Don't be. Mr. Alson's a fine fellow, and I've been told he's mentored many a blossoming artist. The Creator gives us talents to show His beauty, and He wants us to use them, not keep them hidden or tucked away. Right now, my creative purpose is to make this island as beautiful as it can be, but who knows what the future might bring to me? Or to you?"

Colleen's brows furrowed. "That's what Mr. Alson said." She paused and turned to him. "Enough about me. A penny for your thoughts?"

Jack blew out a mournful sigh. "It's Austria. Some Bosnian Serb student assassinated the Archduke Franz Ferdinand and his wife last week, on June 28th. I just read about it in the papers. Shot them in cold blood. The archduke was to take the throne, but now... I fear the subversive act may bring on war."

Colleen furrowed her brow. "How tragic, but I don't understand. How could a murder lead to war?"

He combed his hair with his fingers from his forehead to the nape of his neck before answering. "It may set off a chain of events that could change our world. There's a complex web of alliances in Europe—and all around the globe—that, I fear, might decide that a world war is in their best interests. If so, Austria would be at the very center."

She rolled her hands around each other over and over, her eyes growing wide. "Oh, dear. Will your family be in danger?"

"I'm afraid so."

Champ scampered up and joined them just then, interrupting their conversation. But what more could Jack say? He knew little else about the matter until the newspapers reported on the issue or he received letters from home. Yet, after she listened with the empathy he sought, his worries fluttered away on the breeze. At least for the moment.

The moon rose slowly as they petted and played with the mutt. Colleen laughed at his antics, and his heart swelled at her light-heartedness, a joy he'd not seen before. Perhaps she wasn't the broken soul she seemed.

She quirked a brow and grinned. "May I ask a rather strange question?"

"Certainly."

Her face scrunched up with what might be a touch of self-reproof. "Is Mrs. Lacey smitten with Mr. Alson? I've seen her look at him…"

Jack ducked his chin, a small chuckle spilling over his lips. "I know the look, but no. She's just taken with his fame. Last week, I took her to the bay, and she just about swooned when she mentioned his upcoming visit. Some people fawn over people of prominence, but the truth is, we're all just… people. Still, she's a wonderful woman. Dedicated to Mrs. Clark's welfare."

Colleen agreed. "I do like her. And him."

"Me too."

Wait. Is Colleen smitten with the artist?

Jack threw a stick larger than his forearm. It landed in the water, and Champ jumped in to fetch it. When he brought it back to him, the dog dropped it and shook a shower of river water off his fur and onto them.

Colleen giggled. "You silly dog. You've got us all wet."

She wiped her face with her shirtsleeve, but her smile beamed with mirth. The sight was more magical than the sunset.

Jack continued to toss the stick but avoided the water. No need to make a mess of the lovely *fraulein* or cause her to leave. "With all the upheaval and rumors, many would expect me to hide my Austrian-German heritage, but I refuse. And you needn't be ashamed of your Irish heritage, you know. We are who God made us to be. We needn't be victims of our circumstances. When we put our faith in God, we can be victors over them."

He held his breath, hoping she would accept his simple admonition.

Her brow furrowed deep, her eyes taking on the sadness he'd seen before. "Brave words, but you do not know what I've been through, Irish heritage or not. I'm not sure God gives a whit about me or my heritage, my past, or my future. But at present, I need to get back to my room or I may find my future in peril. Thank you for the walk."

Jack stood and offered her his hand. "My pleasure. I'll walk you back."

A comfortable silence filled their hike back to Comfort cottage. What was she thinking about the turn of conversation?

He thought only of that—and her.

And he prayed.

CHAPTER 7

Days later, Colleen hung the last towel on the line to dry. Towel Day was the bane of her work week. They were hard to wash, tough to rinse, even tougher to roll, and heavy to hang. She arched her aching back.

Since her first meeting with Mr. Alson, he still hadn't beckoned her to show him her sketches. But the lapsing days helped her gather her nerves and find her resolve—a strength that almost bordered on excitement. Indeed, to her surprise, she actually wanted the artist's professional opinion.

She surveyed her day's work, more than a dozen towels billowing in the breeze. She'd become quite proficient in her job, even enjoying the solitude, especially when other duties occupied Marshall. The woman was like sandpaper on a baby's bottom, and she despised the very sight of her.

"Good afternoon, Miss Sullivan." As if conjured by her thoughts, Mr. Alson appeared from behind the line of towels. "Looks like you've done a full day's work. Might you have time for a chat?"

Colleen let out a startled chuckle and smiled. "Perfect timing, sir. I just finished."

Mr. Alson beamed, sweeping an arm toward the main channel of the river. "That's providential. Why don't you fetch your drawings and meet me channelside?"

"Sir, I happen to have them here. I've been bringing them with me every day in case you wanted to see them." Colleen's cheeks grew warm at her admission. She fled to the laundry house, gathered her wits and her portfolio, and returned to the fresh outdoors. A giggle escaped her lips. "Here they are."

Mr. Alson nodded toward the shore. "Shall we?"

When they settled at the same spot where she'd captured her sailboat sketch, she turned to that sketch. "I drew this from here."

Colleen bit her bottom lip, fingering her apron to calm her jitters.

Mr. Alson stared at the drawing for a long while, glancing at the river and back at her sketch. Back and forth. Forth and back until she thought she'd burst with angst.

"What were you doing drawing in such a tempest? The gathering storm appears ominous. I know the river storms well, and they're no place to be sketching." His furrowed brow punctuated his concern. "That could have been dangerous."

Colleen chuckled. "Oh, it was a sunny day. I just imagined the storm."

"And the sailboat? Did you imagine that, too?"

"No, it passed by right there." She pointed to the spot etched in her mind. "But it moved on before I could finish the sketch. I drew from memory."

Mr. Alson studied the drawing again. "Exquisite. You have a rare talent, miss, just as Jack declared." He thumbed the pages of her handmade portfolio as he appraised her with eyes that seemed to beg her indulgence. But he didn't turn the pages. Her heart swelled with jubilation at his compliment and his respect for her work. "May I?"

Colleen sucked in a breath and dipped her chin, glancing at the portfolio, beckoning him to continue to critique her work. Excited to.

A contented sigh left his lips, and he turned to the beginning, studying the same sketches Jack had seen—the sunset, the wrens, the tree grove, the muskrat. But since then, Colleen had filled her notebook with a dozen more drawings. A huge freighter, longer than the island, consuming the page. The laundry line of sheets aglow in the setting sun. Squirrels scampering along the pathway to the cottage. And more.

Mr. Alson took his time studying each one, almost reverently, before turning the page to view the next one. He softly chuckled a few times and mumbled a "hmmm..." or "ahhh..." several times. But she couldn't read his thoughts worth a chicken's liver.

When he flipped through the empty pages, his lips turned downward. He looked at her for several moments before affirming them. "May I comment? Please?"

Did he not like them? Would he criticize her work like all the others had? Her heart thumped alarm, a lump forming in her throat. She swallowed it and consented.

Mr. Alson turned back to the sunset, running his hand over the drawing. "Do you only use pencil? Have you ever played with color?"

"I haven't, sir. Though I'd like to try." She peeked at her sketch. She'd hoped to capture the hues of yellows, oranges, reds with shades of gray. She'd imagined the blue sky turning purple. But she only had a pencil. Nothing more. No money to buy colored ones.

Mr. Alson broke into her misgivings. "I can see the sunset. *Feel* it. Even in monochrome. Do you realize what you have here?" He took her hand in his and stroked her fingers. "Few can achieve such beauty with one color, especially gray."

He let go of her hand and turned the page. "When I was just a boy, a family friend, Helen Balfour, inspired me to pursue art. Who inspired you?"

Colleen blew out a breath. Now he'd know what an amateur she really was. So be it. "No one, sir. I must draw or I'll burst."

"I understand completely, and I concur." Mr. Alson admitted. "I received classical training here in America and in France, but I have since adapted a form of French Impressionism using the *en plein air* technique—which simply means that I like to paint my landscapes in the great outdoors instead of inside a stuffy studio."

Colleen chuckled. "I enjoy drawing outside, too. The light is so much richer and real."

Mr. Alson turned to her tree grove drawing. "I can see that. And your laundry billowing in the sunset?" He turned to the sketch and tapped it. "I'd love to see this in watercolor."

He closed the portfolio and handed it to her, his dark eyes soft, a gentle smile crossing his lips. He bobbed his chin, almost imperceptibly. Could it be admiration—or dismissal?

He stood and put out his hand. "Come. I want to show you something."

Colleen blinked. He had nothing else to say? No advice or further comments? She'd expected more. Criticism. Caution. A critique or judgment that would help her learn.

She sighed, stood, and followed him to the cottage. What else could he do? He was the son of Mrs. Clark.

Before entering the house, Mr. Alson stopped and winked at her. "You should see the works of James McNeill Whistler. His work influenced mine a great deal."

He didn't wait for her to respond but led her into the cottage and up to the second floor. "Wait here a moment. I want to show you my Panama Canal paintings."

Mr. Alson disappeared into one of the five bedrooms and promptly returned with two large, framed paintings.

His excitement was palpable. "When I read about the Panama Canal, I felt compelled to paint it. It took some doing, but I convinced the powers that be to let me go down into the excavation site and paint. Sometimes I feared it might cost me my life, but I wanted to capture the innovation and human investment of this project. I completed more than a dozen." He wiggled the piece of art in his right hand before leaning it against the wall. "I call this one, *In the Cut*. What do you think?"

Colleen studied the painting for several minutes before responding. She wanted to *experience* the painting. "Oh, Mr. Alson, I've only ever read about the Panama Canal, but I could never picture it. And now I feel as if I'm in the middle of the excavation. I can smell the muddy dirt and feel the heat. I hear the clatter of the machinery and smell the coal burning on the train. And I sense the danger of the project. I've read that many people perished during its construction, correct?"

His somber sigh agreed. "My, but you're an astute woman. How do you know so much?"

"I love to read as well as draw. I pick newspapers out of the rubbish bin and read them from cover to cover." She shrugged and turned back to the painting, pointing to two spots in the masterpiece. "Here and here you've captured the light so well. Yet somehow, your subtle use of blue, green, and purple pastels transforms the busy construction site into a rather serene setting."

Mr. Alson's eyes danced with delight. "Astonishing. Thank you, miss. I appreciate your insightful appraisal." He turned to the second painting. "This is *The San Miguel Locks, Panama.* Your thoughts on this one?"

His affirmation gave her the courage to continue, but she examined it for several moments before commenting. "This painting is so utterly intricate. Little people busy at work amidst the giant industrial machinery that dwarfs them. The massive canal walls and colossal gates." She paused and assessed it further. "I can almost hear the supervisors shout in Spanish, ordering their crew to work harder. Yet, I also sense the importance of the project. The clashing sights of mammoth construction against the smallness of man screams of sacrifice, humility, and wonder."

"You've captured the very heart of what I strived to create. Thank you for putting it into words so eloquently. Only a true artist's heart could articulate the intricacies of another painter's work as you have." Mr. Alson plunged his hands into his pockets and exhaled. He reminded her of a little boy, praised until he blushed. For a long while, he stared at her as if making a mighty important decision before pointing toward the end of the hallway. "I want you to help me finish the German village. Tomorrow."

Colleen sucked in a breath and slowly blew it out. "I cannot. I've never painted. Only sketched. I'd ruin it."

Mr. Alson shook his head. "I disagree. I believe you have untapped potential that's begging to burst forth. Don't worry. I'll guide you."

Between the village painting and where she and Mr. Alson stood, a door slowly creaked open. Marshall stepped into the hallway, blocking Colleen's view of the German village. The woman planted herself between the art and them, folding her arms over her chest and glaring at her with a boldness that shocked her. In front of Mr. Alson. The scowl and her narrowed glare meant only one thing.

Trouble.

~ ~ ~

Jack hadn't seen such a wide, blissful smile on Colleen's face, well, ever. She fairly glowed, and it wasn't yet sunset. When she noticed him waving her to join him, she smiled brightly and picked up her step.

He motioned for her to sit. "Good evening, *Fraulein*. And what has you all aglow this evening? You glistened all throughout dinner, and that pretty smile is still playing on your lips."

Colleen settled on a tree stump facing the New York mainland. "Mr. Alson appraised my sketches and liked them."

Jack chuckled. "Liked them? My guess is that you're being modest. And you worried about his critique." He gave her a bobbing eyebrow for good measure.

133

She hung her head, and the shadow of sadness returned. "I've never had positive reviews—until now."

"Those prior critics are *dummkopfs*." He rolled his eyes. "Idiots. Blind to talent. Or jealous. Or just plain mean."

The oaks, maples, and birch around them trembled in the wind sweeping off the river, as if applauding his declaration. "You have a gift, Colleen, as I'm sure Mr. Alson confirmed."

She shrugged, her chocolate pools of delight melting at his words. "But I've no training. I'll never be more than I am without proper education."

Jack harrumphed. "It doesn't matter. God created you to create. That's rather obvious. But you're poor, as I am. In the Bible, James wrote about our predicament. He said that God chose the poor in the world to be rich."

Colleen's brow furrowed, and she tilted her head. "How can that be? I barely own the clothes on my back. I don't even have a set of colored pencils."

He waved an arm wide. "But look at what you've already created. And this place. Whether rich or poor, you and I get to enjoy the wonder of it. And sometimes, we who don't have all the frippery of the wealthy life learn to appreciate the wonders of nature. Often the rich have so many distractions that they miss the beauty of God's creation. Nor do they hear His still, small voice in the cacophony of social expectations. They don't have to rely on their faith for the very bread they eat. Don't you see? We are rich in what *really* matters."

"That may be so, but they cannot teach me the skills I need to grow in my art." She griped, folding her arms over her chest like a toddler refusing a cookie. "I'll forever just be sketching when I'm not ironing, mending, or doing laundry."

"Trust the Creator with your talent and see what He might do." His stalwart tone surprised him—and her. He'd meant to be softer. Gentler. "He never wastes His workmanship."

Colleen narrowed her eyes and raised her chin. Had he said too much? Pushed too hard? For several moments neither spoke, so he took the time to pray she'd understand what he was trying to say. Her countenance grew sadder and sadder.

"Marshall saw me talking with Mr. Alson. She was livid." Her voice trembled at her disclosure. "What shall I do? She's my supervisor, but he's Mr. Clark. He wants me to paint with him tomorrow, but she'll try to stop me. I know she will."

So that was what upset her. Not him.

Jack clicked his tongue, anger surging through his veins. That woman. "The Clarks own this island. Therefore, Mr. Clark has precedence over anything Mrs. Marshall says or does. Just you mind that. Even so, I'm sorry you're caught in the middle."

Colleen squinted toward the far shore, her face turning white. Her eyes widened, and she pointed toward the mainland. "Who are they?"

Jack smiled and waved. "Algonquin Indians. Late last night, Captain Comstock and I went ashore to settle them down. Seems a few of the braves had a little too much fire water before leaving on their big hunt. Did you hear them? They were whooping up quite a racket, but when we asked them to simmer down, the chief courteously sent them to their teepees."

Colleen's eyebrows danced. "Really? I've never seen real Indians before. Only pewter ones we played with in the orph..."

Jack continued. "Seems these Thousand Islands are sacred grounds to the Iroquois and Algonquins. The owner of the property, William Dewart, allows them to use the land and the spring that's on it as they pass through the area."

He stood and pulled arrowheads from a pocket, pressing one into her palm. "Keep this. I have others."

She studied it, turning it over in her hand. "Thank you, Jack. This is a special gift."

But she turned her attention back to the three braves standing on the shore. Each had several feathers in their headband and wore fringed buckskin, but no shirt. One had stripes of red and black on his face and chest.

"Why do they paint themselves like that?"

Such a curious *fraulein*. He liked that. Liked her. "I asked Captain that, too. It's a form of mental conditioning. They use crushed roots, berries, and tree bark to paint themselves. They think it holds magical powers to protect them when they go hunting or into battle. I expect these young braves will be hunting game tonight."

Colleen murmured little more than a "hmmm...." Then she pulled a small pad of paper and nub of a pencil from her pocket and furiously sketched, as if he weren't sitting next to her. As if they weren't in the middle of a conversation. As if she were enchanted. She licked her lips, sucked in her bottom lip, and chewed the end of her pencil as she studied them.

He witnessed magic at work. It reminded him of the hours he'd spend watching his *opa* create his art on the buildings of Vienna. His grandfather once admitted that the muse would catch him in a near frenzy until he captured what he imagined. Was that what he saw now?

He studied the Indians standing at attention, the sun bright and strong on their faces, as if waiting for her to finish. Then he surveyed her sketch. "Incredible. How do you do that? You not only capture the visual aspects of what we're seeing but also the very essence of their character. Strong. Brave. Fearless."

She smiled, giving her appreciation for the affirmation. "Someday I'll paint them."

The determination in her tone set his heart afire. "I'm sure you will."

Mrs. Marshall's deep, angry voice carried on the breeze, dispelling the magic of the moment. "Miss Sullivan. Come here at once."

Colleen dropped her pencil and gasped. "Coming." The alarm on her ashen face unnerved him. She scrambled to her feet and stuck the pad in her pocket. "I'm in hot water now."

Jack tucked himself behind a tree, hoping Mrs. Marshall hadn't seen her with him. He observed Colleen's retreat to the laundry house, a sense of dread building in his heart. From where he hid, he had an unobstructed view of the angry woman raving and railing at Colleen. He could only hear the rumble of her words, but he knew they were nefarious and cruel by the wicked look on her face. Then she grabbed

Colleen's arms and jerked her, threw her off balance, and sent her tumbling to the ground.

Mrs. Marshall's face was as red as the thorny redbuds on a nearby bush. She hollered, "You think that pretty face of yours will save you? Keep away from him, you worthless waif, or you'll be begging for bread on the streets of Alexandria Bay before you can say jack rabbit."

He vowed he'd have Marshall begging for her life if she didn't watch it.

But how?

CHAPTER 8

Colleen set the iron down and rubbed her hip. Thanks to Marshall's angry outburst yesterday, the bruise was as large as a saucer, black and blue, swollen and sore. Her wrist hurt, too, but thankfully it wasn't her left hand, else she wouldn't be able to complete her work. Then where would she be? Locked in the cellar, likely.

"Wretched woman." She mumbled out a breath and picked up the iron, pressing out every wrinkle in Mrs. Clark's creamy damask day dress. "And blast this miserable lace." She chewed her bottom lip, fearful she might burn or tear the intricate, fragile webbing. "God, help me do a good job."

141

She'd done it before. Though the nuns had no finery, Sister Patricia secretly wore lacey pantaloons her brother gave her. The nun snuck them to Colleen and demanded she wash and iron them in absolute privacy. But she was only twelve at the time, and when she put the iron to the delicate lace, it melted before her very eyes. Her reward: a day with a sore bottom, locked in the sweltering attic without food, water, or comfort of any kind. Not even a stub of coal with which to draw. No, the cellar was infinitely better.

She pulled Mr. Alson's trousers from the pile. The tiniest spot of paint brought a smile to her lips, somehow lessening her frustrations. Such a nice man, and so willing to share his expertise and love of art with her. And he'd invited her to help him paint.

Conceivably, she should believe what Mr. Alson and Jack said about her sketches. Both had experience assessing art. But how could everyone else be mistaken? Considering their character—or lack of it— maybe the nuns and orphans were wrong. After all, they'd not had any training in that field.

She ironed the pants, then pressed a dozen plain cotton aprons. But the longer she worked, the worse her hip throbbed, until she could barely stand. Perhaps ice would ease the pain.

Colleen hobbled to the icehouse, just a dozen feet from the laundry, and found the door ajar. She took three steps up into the double-walled round stone icehouse and stepped inside. A delicious chill kissed her face. "Hello. Is someone here?"

Tara's unmistakable voice ended with her signature giggle. "Aye, I'm here. Colleen, is that you?"

Colleen's eyes adjusted to the dark to glimpse her roommate filling a bucket with ice. "Fancy seeing you here. I'm just getting a chunk of ice for my h..."

Tara frowned. "Your head? Are you feeling poorly?"

Should Colleen confide in her roommate or stay silent? Could she trust her? In the past, anytime she'd disclosed her problems, her confession ended up bringing more trouble. Punished for admitting ill treatment hardly seemed fair. But such was her lot.

"It's just hot in the laundry house. A piece of ice is a treat."

Both true—though not why she truly wanted the ice.

Tara picked up her bucket, and Colleen grabbed a chunk of ice the size of her hand, holding it in her apron. They stepped into the bright sunshine, and Tara pulled the door shut. "Do you know that every winter they cut blocks of ice from the river and pack it with sawdust so it lasts all summer? We never run out, even when we have parties galore."

Colleen indicated the tiny nearby canal. "And did you know this used to be a larger cut between the Nemahbin cottage on the far end of the island and Comfort? In 1890, the river current washed a dead body into the canal, so Mrs. Clark demanded the workmen fill the canal so that would never happen again." She paused at the sight of her bewildered roommate. "Jack told me. Can you imagine how much work that would be?"

Tara shook her head and rubbed an arm with her free hand. "That's terrible, but such an interesting story. I hadn't heard." She lifted her ice bucket a few inches. "We're having a dinner party tonight. I mean, Mrs. Clark and Mr. Alson are. The house is abuzz with preparations and excitement."

Colleen smiled. And here she was, stuck out in this place of drudgery. She shifted the ice chunk, letting it fall to the center of her apron like a lady of leisure in a hammock. "That's nice. Enjoy getting ready for the evening. I'll see you at dinner."

"Enjoy your solitude and the great outdoors." Tara touched her right wrist as a friendly gesture. "Perhaps you'll meet a handsome stranger in the garden."

"Ouch." Colleen clamped her lips together. She must hide her pain. "Your hands are icy."

"Not so as to pull a cry like that from a mere tap." Tara set down her bucket and whined. "Please tell me what's ailing you."

Now she'd have to confess. Something. The moment demanded it. With a sigh, Colleen set her ice on a grassy spot in the shade and leaned against the icehouse wall, rubbing her right hand. "I had a minor accident yesterday. I tripped on a rock and landed on my arm."

All true. Sort of.

Tara clicked her tongue and raised an eyebrow. "I'm so sorry. Perhaps you should take the day off. I can let Mrs. Lacey know, and Mrs. Marshall will have to let you rest."

Goodness. What had she done? "No. Please don't tell anyone. Marshall will have me fired, and I need the work."

Tara wrung her hands, concern plastered on her gentle face. "Aye, but only if you're sure. I won't say anything. Still, I will pray for you."

"Thank you. I'll be fine. Please keep this between us."

Tara agreed and picked up her pail.

Colleen scooped up her ice. "We both have work to do. See you later."

Tara trudged up the hill, but she peered back several times. Why had she opened her big mouth and told Tara about her pain? Would her roommate betray her trust?

After icing her hip and wrist, Colleen picked up the iron again. She'd finish her commitment here on the island, but she wouldn't come back. Not with the likes of Marshall around. She'd go west if she had to, and she'd find work that didn't include a vicious taskmaster.

She could sew. Perhaps she could find a dress shop or a manufacturer. Surely, they didn't employ the likes of the ogre. She chuckled at the name she coined for Marshall.

"What's so funny, miss?" Marshall stomped into the laundry house, her hands balled into fists. "Eschewing your labors with that mousy little Tara? You're a worthless slacker, that's what you are. Can't even turn my back on you for a moment without your lazy carcass sitting around, chewing on your cud, when you should be working."

Colleen sucked in a ragged breath and pressed her lips together, refusing to take her bait.

Why does she have to be so mean, so devilish?

She steadied herself, planting her hands firmly on the ironing board. How much more could she take just to keep her position? She'd stay for her aunt. For her art. For now.

"Answer me." The woman stepped closer, a deep growl underscoring her demand. Marshall's glare darted from her face to her hands and back again. Then a smirk slithered onto her face. A glint of evil followed. "Well?"

Before she realized what was happening, Marshall tipped the iron onto Colleen's right hand, the heavy thing burning hot, searing the back of it.

"Ahhh!"

Colleen screeched, pulling the iron off. But it was too late. A fiery red blotch appeared immediately. The searing pain overshadowed her hip and wrist, but she gritted her teeth. She wouldn't cry in front of the ogre, even as blisters formed.

Marshall feigned surprised innocence. "Oh, dear. I'm so sorry." For emphasis, she dramatically put her hand to her bosom. "Did that heavy iron tip onto your hand by mistake?" Her mocking, flat tone infuriated Colleen. "What a terrible accident."

She longed to punch her, kick her. Smash the hot iron in her face. But she'd seen what ogres like her did to someone who crossed them. Poor Sally was never the same after she tried to defend herself against Sister Patricia.

No, she needed the job.

And she'd not give Marshall the satisfaction of victory.

She'd retaliate.

In due time.

~ ~ ~

The next morning at breakfast, Jack gasped at the sight of Colleen's bandaged hand. She'd missed dinner last evening, and he'd not seen her until now. Something was very wrong. Her sadness had returned, and he guessed pain with it. But she was at the end of the table, and he had no chance to talk with her.

Unfortunately, immediately after the meal, Captain whisked him away to town to cart supplies for him, so all morning he was off the island. But he'd find her. He'd find out what happened to the sweet *fraulein*.

Might he attain counsel in Captain? As they shuttled back to the island, he wondered. Though the man always had a smile on his face, somehow, he exuded superiority, an invisible boundary Jack dared not cross. No, he'd have to find a confidant in someone else. But who?

By mid-day, Jack was back on the island, and his angst was at a record high. After seeing the altercation between Mrs. Marshall and Colleen, he hadn't slept all night, stewing about the abuse he'd witnessed. And now the problem with her hand? He couldn't *not* do something, but what?

He turned to his other burden—his homeland. That morning he read Captain's *Watertown Daily Times*, the headlines of war in huge, bold print. His world was turning upside down, in a flux of utter confusion, and he wasn't sure what to do with the information bouncing around in his skull.

He'd do some hard work. That should relieve his churning. Physical activity always seemed to help.

He'd clean out the beach area and shoreline, and hopefully glimpse Colleen. Maybe even find the words to investigate her situation. With a wheelbarrow full of tools, he headed from the boathouse, over the hilly island, and down the steep path past the laundry house and onto the beach. Colleen wasn't at the laundry, but perhaps she'd come soon.

Jack began tidying the tiny beach by readjusting the heavy rocks that surrounded and marked off the sandy area. The river's currents constantly played havoc with them, and a recent storm pulled several out of place.

Once he finished the outside perimeter, he tackled the beach area, cleaning up debris swept in on the tide. Lots of seaweed, moss, dead fish, and a broken oar. While he worked, he wondered at the news of Austria's troubles, and he feared what might come of it. He prayed for the country of his birth, for his family and friends, the farm, the future.

But he wasn't there to help. Tonight, he'd write a letter. Yet how long would it take to get there? Or would it ever arrive?

After pulling up his trouser legs and yanking up his shirtsleeves, he stepped into the cool river and tugged out the seaweed. It was a constant battle to keep the bottom clear of the slimy stuff, but he rather enjoyed the task. He pulled handfuls of the plant until the entire area was free of it. For now. In another few weeks, they'd return, and he'd repeat the process.

He stepped onto the beach and piled the seaweed knew high. Then he carefully raked the sand into a vision of perfection. When he finished, he swiped at the sweat trickling down his face before craning his neck to notice that, in the distance, the laundry room door was open. Perhaps Colleen was there.

Jack harrumphed. He had to deal with the abuse Mrs. Marshall had inflicted on her, but how? How could he inquire about the situation without embarrassing—or infuriating—her? Colleen would have his head if he went around her and addressed the problem directly. He couldn't risk losing the one and only friend he'd found since coming to the country. A friendship he hoped might one day grow into more.

Colleen was a rare gem. A diamond in the rough, as his uncle would say.

He smiled at the comparison as he put his tools back in the wheelbarrow. His uncle, a jeweler, had hired Jack to work for the summer before his *opa* sent him to America. Jack learned much about gems of all kinds. Diamonds were most interesting.

As a diamond, Colleen's color and cut were perfect. Beautiful. Creative. Yes, she had a few pain-filled imperfections—his uncle would call them inclusions. But didn't everyone have some flaw? No one was perfect. He certainly wasn't.

Truth was, he wanted to know what pained her. To understand her. He lay in bed night after night, wondering what held Colleen captive. Praying for her. He'd never seen such sad, beautiful eyes in all his life, and they haunted him. What had scarred her so?

But how could he discover the origin? Time, he suspected, was the only answer.

Yet he had other troubles, too. Just yesterday, war came to his beloved homeland. The paper's headline declared that on "July 28, 1914, Austria-Hungary declares war on Serbia. World War I has begun."

He sucked in a breath. What did they mean by World War? Would the entire globe end up fighting on the soil of his homeland? God forbid.

As he wheeled the barrow up the hill, he returned to the more immediate concern. Colleen. He maneuvered toward the laundry house and found her inside, ironing awkwardly. Her bandaged hand gingerly pulled the tablecloth in place.

He cleared his throat so not to frighten her. "*Grüss Gott*, Colleen. How are you today?"

Jack scolded himself at the rise in his voice. He'd meant for it to be a casual greeting. Why did she fluster him so?

"I'm fine."

Her tone flat, her fleeting glance at him fidgety, guarded. She kept ironing, as if to send him on his way without another word.

"Your hand. It's bandaged. What happened?"

There. He'd crossed the divide.

"An accident with the iron yesterday. I'll be fine."

She still didn't look at him. Still didn't stop working. Still sounded flat. Distant.

Could he question her about Marshall? He must. "Like the accident two days ago when Marshall pushed you?"

Colleen sucked in a breath so loud it alarmed him. Her eyes grew wide, and her face turned ashen. Then red. She squared her shoulders and her eyes narrowed. "I don't know what you think you saw, sir, but it's none of your affair. Please leave me be. And don't probe into areas where you have no business poking your nose." She angled her body away from him. "Good day."

Jack stepped back as if punched. "I only asked because I care, Colleen. No one should treat you so." He paused, drawing a deep breath. Praying she'd listen. "May I share a story with you?"

She shrugged then returned to her work. "I suspect I couldn't stop you if I wanted."

Well, that was something at least.

"A magnificent bald eagle nested near here, just across the river on Wellesley Island. He soared on the

155

breeze wild and free until one day a great storm blew in and tossed him hither and yon. The tempest broke his wing. By and by, it healed, but he was afraid to fly. He tried over and over, but he'd get only a few feet in the air before giving up. One day, a strong wind blew, and the eagle tried again. The gust took him aloft, and he soared on the breeze, finally free again."

Colleen stopped ironing and glared at him with a furrowed brow. "What's your point? You think I'm broken? Of course, I am. I wouldn't be in this sweltering shack doing what I hate if I weren't. But there's no wind under my wings. Only this." She picked up the heavy iron and waggled it in front of her. "Please leave me be."

"Jack? Is Colleen there?"

Mr. Alson appeared from behind the building. How much had he heard? She'd be livid if she thought he knew her troubles.

"I know that eagle. He's a beauty. Sometimes he'll land on the cottage rooftop and peck at the weathervane bear." Mr. Alson chuckled, poking his head into the laundry house and waving. "Hello, miss. Can you get away and paint with me?"

Colleen sighed. She licked her lips and shook her head. "I'm afraid not today, sir. I have so much to do." She pointed to a pile of napkins and tablecloths. "And with the party tonight, I must finish these."

Mr. Alson shrugged. "No problem. Tomorrow then. We'll have a dandy time finishing that German village."

Jack motioned toward the cottage. "I've been meaning to ask, what's the story behind the weathervane in the form of a life-size bear reaching for the sun on top of the house?"

Mr. Alson chuckled. "He's a novelty, I'll grant you that. But I don't rightly know where the idea came from. I think it was my father's notion." He grew somber before turning to Jack. "Have you seen the papers? Austria and Hungary declared war on Serbia."

Pleased to have someone with whom to discuss the subject, Jack acquiesced. "I read about it today. The article said it could become a world war. My family's there."

"I'm so sorry, Jack. If you need assistance to get back to your family, I'll help." He paused, his fists balled. "If America joins the war, they can count me in. I'll take aerial photography or create paintings of the battles."

Mr. Alson's determination rang in his words, spurring Jack to courage he didn't know he had. "I'd sign up too." Jack plunged his hands in his pockets. "But first, I must inquire about the safety of my family, yet I fear the mail might be a problem."

Colleen let out a tiny moan, causing both men to snap a glance at her. He'd forgotten she was there, listening to the manly discourse.

Jack stepped into the doorway. "Are you all right, *fraulein*?"

An uncertain smile crossed her lips, contrasting with a bleakness in her pretty brown eyes he hadn't seen before.

"Can our world never find peace?"

Jack shrugged. "Probably not."

She turned back to her ironing. "Then what's the point in it all?"

CHAPTER 9

Standing in the presence of such an accomplished artist and his art the following afternoon, Colleen reiterated her concerns about painting, especially on a Comfort cottage wall. "Sir, I've never painted before. Only sketched. I'd hate to ruin this fine piece of art."

Mr. Alson handed her a palate as if he didn't hear her. He pointed to various elements of the half-completed scene. "Given your proficient work, you probably already know that you look for the shapes, lines, and curves you can observe in nature. Creating something like this is like putting together a puzzle."

She concurred. Exactly how she approached a piece of art.

He showed her the paint and how to mix it to form various colors and hues. He pointed out which brushes she should use for different aspects of the work.

"You want to mix the beauty of various colors so they will expose themselves within the different hues. Don't worry, Miss Sullivan. I'll be by your side and will guide you along the way."

Her neck warmed under her collar. Colleen sighed, sucking in her bottom lip and shifting nervously from foot to foot. Her uncertainty must've been evident, for Mr. Alson's brows narrowed. He took her hands in his, gazing at the bandage and shaking his head.

His coffee-brown eyes almost hid his pupils, so dark and deep they were. "Are you left-handed?"

Her hands quivered as she tried to quell her trepidation, but to no avail. "Yes."

His clean-shaven face had tiny, black dots of stubble darkening his jawline. "Being left-handed is a sign of artistic propensities."

Really? The nuns had smacked her hand when she used it, claiming it was a mental deficiency she must overcome. A ripple of hope edged through her mind, scaring her more than Timmy, the orphanage's meanest bully. She pasted on a grateful smile.

Mr. Alson grew somber, his gaze lugubrious. "I see someone has hurt you. I see it even more in your eyes. In your countenance." He paused, staring at her, compassion filling his eyes. "The tapestry of one's life often has dark threads that can bring out the lighter, deeper beauty. If you let it."

She shuddered under his discerning gaze. She nodded, then shrugged. It was as if he could see into her very soul. She sucked in a breath and held it.

"Paint the scars, Miss Sullivan. Don't flee from them. Don't shun them. Embrace them so you can be free to soar. They will give you power to create in a way that little else can. Hurts and scars and shadows of the past can generate hues that bring your art to life. Without pain, we are one-dimensional creatures who have little to share."

His words were as gentle as a kitten's lick, yet as powerful as a lion's roar.

Mr. Alson drew her hands close to his face as if he intended kissing them. Instead, he gave her fingertips a gentle squeeze. "These hands hold the creativity God gave you. No one else has the gift you have. No one ever will." He let go of her hands and stepped back. "Paint the scars."

Colleen feasted her teary eyes on the art before her, even as she trembled under his words, under his keen insight. Hope flickered, a tiny flame burgeoning inside her, spreading into the corners of her thoughts, dispelling the pain of the past, awakening a dream of what might be.

"Shall we begin?" Mr. Alson sketched a bridge over a moat and the beginnings of a grassy lawn in the foreground. "Why don't you start here?"

He rubbed his hand over the bridge. After showing her which brush and paint to use, he demonstrated how to layer texture and dimension with a variety of short and long brushstrokes. Then he climbed a nearby ladder and created a banner over the entire painting.

As Colleen tentatively swept her brush over the bridge, Mr. Alson chatted like a lifelong friend. "You mentioned you're from Watertown? In 1901, I rented a barn there from a friend's parents and converted it into an art studio. It marked the beginning of my professional career, and it's where I met my precious wife, Medora. She posed as my model, with her mother by her side. Soon, we fell in love and married on September 20, 1902. She has been my muse ever since."

Colleen flinched at his personal confession. "That's so touching. Where is she now?"

Mr. Alson waved a hand. "She's been visiting with family, but she will be here this weekend. She's been a supportive partner in my work, organizing my first solo exhibition in Watertown and many more since." Mr. Alson paused and surveyed her work. "You're doing a splendid job, my dear. Shade in a little darker gray here and here." From his perch above, he indicated the spots where the sun would naturally cast shadows, and then he promptly returned to sketching in a banner that read ALT NEMOBERG.

He put his pencil down and painted it. "After that, we took my paintings to Chicago for my first major exhibition at the Anderson Galleries. I received positive reviews from famous critics, bolstering my confidence." He stopped his work and turned to her, waiting for her to cease and look at him. When she did, he smiled. "I expect you'll experience such praise one day."

Colleen giggled, shaking her head in utter disbelief. "Me? Never. I only sketch for fun."

Mr. Alson climbed down the ladder, slipped the brush from her fingers, and took her left hand. "Miss Sullivan, you underestimate your gift. Is it not God who gave you this talent? You must grasp every opportunity to grow in the craft and show God's handiwork through you."

Talent? Craft? God's handiwork? Surely not. It was a hobby. Yes, she loved it. She even obsessed over it. But was this God's doing?

He climbed the ladder and returned to his work—and his story—as if he had never tossed her the epiphany she just received. "After we married, we moved to Paris and made friends with notable American artists who lived there, then we traveled around Europe. I aligned my work with Impressionist practices and grew in the craft."

He pointed his brush at her. "You know, Miss Sullivan, fellow artists can help you grow in your craft. Becoming a professional artist is a journey that takes years to accomplish, but I hope you'll count on me as a fellow artist in your journey."

A tiny moan escaped Colleen's trembling lips. This was all too much to take in. Her, a fellow artist with *him*? "Th... thank you, sir. You are." With paint brush aloft, she bowed in humble gratitude.

Mr. Alson bobbed his chin and smiled. "The bridge looks good. Add a few horizontal lines to hint at the texture."

Colleen's brow furrowed. "Sir?"

He climbed down and studied the work, patiently showing her what he meant. "And see how the darker shading in the tunnel entryways gives depth and perspective? Let's do a little more of that underneath the bridge's archway, okay?"

Like a lightning bolt exploding in her brain, she understood. "I see! The sun doesn't hit there, so it must be darker. And the tiny lines make it look like stonework. How interesting."

Mr. Alson chuckled. "I knew you'd catch on quickly. Continue."

Colleen did, and with gusto. Her brush fairly flew into action, taking over her hand like something possessed it. She chewed her bottom lip, concentrating on the art, assessing the exact shading she needed to replicate the shadows, layering color a little at a time. The experience was… delightful.

Mr. Alson laughed with abandon, a twinkle in his eye as he looked down at her. "I love seeing the muse seize an artist."

"I see you're a-mused."

Colleen chuckled at her play on words, feeling like she was soaring on the wings of her brush. Like the bald eagle Jack spoke about. Could she escape the manacles of her past to create with abandon? Could she find life beyond her bonds to accomplish her dreams?

Mr. Alson broke into her reverie. "We returned to Chicago four years ago after I painted dozens of pieces in Spain. And then, last year, I painted the Panama pictures you saw."

She finished the bridge and studied the sketches of the water in the moat. "These rounded lines. Are they to show the shadows of the bridge in the water?"

"Very astute, my dear. Exactly." He stepped down from the ladder and pointed to his sketching. "And here, see how the reflection follows the arched tunnel where the maiden stands?"

Colleen sighed. She could envision it perfectly. "I do. Thank you, sir."

"You've done a masterful job of the bridge. Let's see what you do with the water."

He showed her which colors to mix, touched her shoulder gently, and smiled before returning to his perch on the ladder. He sketched several clouds and what looked to be a cathedral.

"How do you know when you've completed a piece? I see you're adding more to this already beautiful scene."

"Ah, that's an acquired ability. Sometimes you must let it sit awhile, like I did with this scene. I knew it needed more, but I wasn't sure what. Then, last summer, we closed up the cottage before I could decide." He sighed. "I think it was waiting for *you*."

A tiny sigh bubbled out of her, like the coo of a well-fed baby. This man, this famous artist, filled her soul with hope she'd never known.

The nuns had called her an imbecile, dim-witted, feeble-minded, and she believed them. Until she drew. Until she put her thoughts on paper in pictures and sketches. Then she came alive.

And now she soared with a hope for her future she'd not believed possible.

Until now.

~ ~ ~

Jack slipped in beside Colleen, where she perched with her sketchbook, a pencil firmly between her teeth. He stepped on a dry twig and made it crack so not to surprise her with his presence. He motioned to the rock outcropping where she sat. "May I?"

As if coming out of a trance, she blinked. Then she sat up straight and yielded, her dainty features in stark contrast to her will. What gave her the backbone of steel to withstand Marshall's ire and the incessant doldrums of the laundry? What cemented her in a protective casing that nothing could penetrate? She encompassed a mystery he felt compelled to solve. Somehow. Some day.

Colleen turned to a page in her book and carefully slipped it out. "I have something for you. As a peace offering. I'm sorry I was prickly." Colleen handed him the sketch of the three Indians they had seen on the mainland hillside. Around it she'd drawn a framework of arrowheads.

Jack studied the fine pencil drawing for a long while. Then he tapped the paper. "Such talent you have. Thank you. I'll treasure this always."

Her smile tentative, she turned to stare at the view of the river.

The fiery sunset ignited the sky with an effervescent warmth that kissed her cheeks. They sat still and quiet, the silent spell broken only by the crickets and bullfrogs. On the August winds, dark clouds rode upon colorful chariots.

Colleen glowed in the pumpkin light. "I love the river more and more each day. When I draw it, I am swept up in its majesty and wonder."

She turned to her latest drawing, a serene rendering of the landscape before them. In the foreground, a fish jumped, its mouth open to catch its dinner.

"You amaze me, *fraulein*. Truly."

Just then, Colleen seemed one with the beauty of the river—yet not. Something hidden in the deep recesses of her being hung there like moss entwined in the propellors of a fine yacht. How could he untangle it?

Jack agreed with her admiration of the St. Lawrence. "Sometimes the river gurgles and coos like a happy infant. Other times, it growls like an angry bear. Sometimes it groans like an old man after a long winter's nap. And other times, it dances like a fair young maiden after her first kiss. The Saint Lawrence River is like that. You can't tame her, for she's wild and free."

"Like the bald eagle?" Colleen searched his face, her gentle eyes fringed with dark lashes, long and thick. "Your eloquence paints a pretty picture, sir."

She'd listened to his tale of the bird? Perhaps he could break through to the formidable *fraulein* after all. "Like the magnificent bald eagle. You're as beautiful as an eagle soaring on a St. Lawrence sunset. I can't wait to see you fly even higher, Colleen."

His thoughts had tumbled from his heart to his lips before he could catch them. His pulse hammered wildly as he sucked in a breath, wishing he could retract the premature confession. But he couldn't. So, he waited—for her to gasp and flee.

She didn't. Something had changed.

"Thank you." A rosy flush moved from her neck to her high cheekbones. She put her unhurt hand to her face, but a dubious smile crossed her lips, as if she'd swallowed a fish that tickled her insides. "No one has ever told me that. Ever."

Sweat misted his brow. "I... it's true..." He smoothed a hand over his short, curly hair, running it all the way back to the nape of his neck. The habit soothed him. Better to change the topic. For now. He cleared his throat. "Tell me about your time painting with Mr. Alson. I heard you completed the village."

Her wistful gaze followed the gulls across the water, and she toyed with an errant curl. "It was magical, as if the brush had a mind of its own. And Mr. Alson taught me so much about mixing colors and using the right brush and the techniques he uses to make it realistic. He even complimented my work. I hope, one day, to try my hand at painting again, for it was the most enchanting day of my life. But the hard, cold reality is that I'll never be able to explore the depths of it on a lowly laundry maid's salary."

Jack's voice rumbled low. "You never know what the future holds. But I know Who holds the future."

"And what does your future hold, Jack? Will you return to Austria to fight in the war or stay here and make a life in America?"

Colleen's brow revealed worries of someone quite her senior. As if she cared about him. As if he really mattered.

He sighed, leaning forward, and planting his forearms on his raised knees. "I sent a letter to my family, but I'm not sure if or when they will get it. The postal service may be a low priority at a time like this. I read Germany had already invaded Luxembourg and Belgium. Seems all of Europe is a chessboard with pawns falling left and right. What's next?"

Colleen patted his hand, sending a shot of warmth up his arm and into his heart. "Lord only knows. But I hope you stay. You've become a good friend, Jack."

He assented, his heart soaring on the breeze but landing all too soon. "I feel that way, too. But to be honest, I don't know what to do. How to go on. If I stay here, I may never see my family or my homeland again. If I go, my life may end sooner rather than later. I feel like I have one foot in Paradise yet feel almost obliged to step into Hades. For my nieces and nephews. For the country of my birth."

Colleen raised her chin high and pulled her shoulders back, an air of mysterious strength exuding from her. Yet, he thought it a facade to cover deeper issues yet unknown. "Oh, please don't go. You have a right to be afraid of what looms over there. Of war. You'd be fodder for the cannons, Jack. Besides, your family insisted you start a new life here, right? So, why would that change now?"

His throat cinched tighter than a nun's wimple. He pointed to her and then to him and back again. "Whatever this is between you and me, I'd like us to discover its depth and find its purpose. Perhaps here I've found my home."

"There you are, Miss Sullivan." Mrs. Marshall stood behind them, arms folded over her chest, her deep manly voice menacing. "You've work to do. The missus has a torn hemline that needs mending. Now."

How long had she been there? What had she heard?

The woman gave Jack a narrow-eyed glare, the ridge between her thick brows forming ugly train tracks. "And what are you doing with the likes of him, the gardener? Utterly inappropriate, except for a floozy."

Jack cast Marshall a nasty glare, scrambled to his feet, and held out his hand to Colleen, but she refused it. Instead, she rolled onto her knees and stood on her own. Retrieving her sketchpad, she held it tight to her chest, eyes downcast, her formidable spirit deflating like a popped balloon.

"What do you have there? Hand it to me."

Mrs. Marshall put out her hand, demanding Colleen relinquish her precious possession to the likes of a monster. She held it tighter, not giving way to the woman.

Jack stepped between them. "We were simply watching the sunset. And that book is hers."

Marshall exploded like a fiery dragon taking flight. "Who are you to talk to me like that? You're nothing but a poor, good-for-nothing kraut, and you will not speak to me that way."

She swung her arm wide and backhanded him with all her might, stinging his cheek and bloodying his nose.

Words imprisoned in his throat surged through his veins like an inferno. He unclenched a fist, pulling a handkerchief from his pocket and thrusting it to his nose to stop the bleeding. He bit his tongue. Here on this tiny island, she was much higher in the pecking order.

Mrs. Marshall's scowl claimed victory as she snapped a glare at him and violently snatched Colleen's sketchbook from her hands. She flipped through its pages and snapped it shut.

"Childish hen scratching, you no good mick. Come with me. Now."

Jack's voice rose in a trembling question. "Who are you to judge her work, ma'am? She's a talented artist."

Mrs. Marshall guffawed, throwing her head back like a wild wolf calling its pack to pounce. "An artist? That's the most ridiculous thing I've ever heard. This sniveling snit isn't worth the air she breathes."

The woman glared at them like a demon possessed. "This is what I think of her art." With all her might, she heaved it into the river.

Jack's heart dropped to his toes as it slipped beneath the waves.

Gone.

CHAPTER 10

Colleen's heart still ached as she remembered how her art plummeted to the bottom of the river. Yet, after her transformative experience of painting with Mr. Alson just four days ago, her life would never be the same. No matter what Marshall—or others of her ilk—said or did.

Her days since fell into a mundane pattern like they had at the orphanage. Her back ached as she stirred the bedsheets in water hot enough to scald. Then she gave them a cool rinse and put them through the ringer. Her raw hands chafed as she hung the bedding.

That was nothing new. When she was but ten, the nuns sent her to work in the orphanage's laundry, spending entire days there until her tiny hands bled and her tired body barely had strength to make it to her bed.

And here? It was much the same, though not as constant. And the lash not as frequent.

Here she had time to draw. Time to think. Time to dream.

But then Marshall destroyed her sketchbook, her prized possession. What would she do? Retaliate? Start over? Give up?

After belaboring her frustrations from sunup to sundown, she'd climbed into bed and fell into a fitful sleep, one that gave no comfort.

Colleen's chest heaved with exertion. She had to get away, but a crooked-toothed ogre chased her through a foreboding, dark forest, the groundcover thick with prickers and thorns, ripping her dress, bloodying her legs. She stumbled and fell into the bramble patch, the barbs jabbing her hands and arms. She tried to rise, but the menacing vines held onto her

like the chains of a prisoner. She couldn't breathe.
Couldn't speak. Would she die in this horrid place?

"Wake up, Colleen." Tara shook her shoulders,
her voice trembling with concern. "You're having a
bad dream. You were whimpering and talking in your
sleep. But it's all right now. Pay it no heed. You're
safe."

Colleen blinked away the nightmare, the early
morning sun casting eerie shadows on the wall. She
wiped the sweat from her brow and sat up, taking a few
deep breaths to calm herself. "What? What did you
say?"

Tara sat on her bed, rubbing her arm. "You cried
out in your sleep, begging someone not to send you
back to the orphanage. To save you from the nuns."

Colleen moaned, pulling her knees to her chest,
wrapping her arms around them, burying her face in
the gap. "Please don't tell anyone that I'm an orphan."

Tara put her hand on her shoulder and gave it a
tender squeeze. "I already knew. Remember?"

Colleen's head popped up, blood rushing to it.
"You did?"

Her roommate gave her a tentative smile. "I suspected, anyway. From things you've said. But it's okay. It's 1914, for heaven's sake, and I don't give a whit where someone comes from. It's what's in their heart and how they behave that matters."

Colleen sucked in a breath, swallowing her surprise. "Really?" She suppressed a whimper. "Even so, please keep this private. Marshall *would* care, and she'd use it against me. Somehow."

Tara conceded. "Aye. Your secret's safe with me."

~ ~ ~

By mid-afternoon, Colleen's knuckles whitened around the handle of the basket, heavy with mending. Whenever she wasn't washing, hanging laundry to dry, or ironing, there was always something to mend.

As she worked, she sat on the back porch in the warm afternoon breeze. Large, puffy clouds raced across the heavens, the summer's heat dissipating on the wings of the wind. She brushed an errant curl from her face, then ran her fingertips over the intricate lace that needed mending.

181

"Are you Miss Sullivan?"

The elegant lady who rounded the path had to be Mr. Alson's wife. Colleen heard she'd arrived, but had yet to see her.

Colleen stood, pantaloons hanging from her hand, her needle dangling from the thread. She curtsied. "I am, ma'am."

The woman stepped onto the porch, motioned her to sit, and pulled up a nearby chair. "Do you mind if I join you? I'm Mr. Alson's wife. You can call me Mrs. Medora."

Are artists and their wives always so unconventional?

Colleen nodded, a measure of curiosity coursing through her veins. "Of course. Your husband has been a generous benefactor with his time and talents."

Mrs. Medora's gentle smile and sparkling gray eyes lit her face. "I've heard he's found a kindred spirit in you, a fellow artist that he finds quite a curiosity. Perhaps even a prodigy."

A prodigy? Poppycock.

Colleen trailed her finger over the pantaloon's spoiled tatting, her spirit somehow melding into it, as if she were that fine, damaged lace. Like this needlework, her art might be creative, but would her past forever blemish it?

She chewed her bottom lip, breathing in and out. She had no response for this kind woman. She couldn't argue her point, but she couldn't agree with it either, so she just shrugged, picked up her needle, and continued sewing.

Mrs. Medora released a tiny sigh. "I'd like to tell you about the women artists who have come before you. Do you mind?"

Colleen appraised this fine lady, her ginger hair coifed perfectly, elegant jewels around her neck, a pale-yellow damask day dress covering her curvy frame. Mrs. Medora waited for an answer with folded hands.

Colleen smiled. "Please. I'd be ever so grateful."

Mr. Alson's wife beamed. "Most of the women artists I've met live in Paris, but there are a few here in America. In fact, there's a women's art institute opening in Chicago this very year. The notable École des Beaux-Arts didn't open its doors to women until 1897. Before that, only a few teachers entertained private studios for ladies. At the Académie Julian, women followed the same art courses as men, though not in the same rooms."

She paused while a large ship passed by the island. "In the art community, women often live together and sketch together in each other's parlors. A few rare husbands support their wives in their work. The Danish painter, Anna Ancher, married a painter, Michael Ancher, and they created their masterpieces side by side."

Colleen listened as she sewed, but she became so engrossed in the woman's story, she pricked her finger. "Ouch." She put her finger to her lips and shrugged, her cheeks warming. "Excuse me, ma'am."

Mrs. Medora chuckled before advancing her monologue. "Yet, even with the support of their family, friends, and fellow painters, women artists face unique challenges. Ladies who hold exhibits in salons or galleries must deal with the world's prejudices and nasty male art critiques. It isn't easy."

She reached over and patted Colleen's hand. "I don't say this to discourage you, dear, but to encourage you that there are many who have already forged a road on which you can walk with the talents God has given you."

Colleen tucked a strand of hair behind her ear. "But I am different, ma'am. My class. My status." She hung her head, ashamed to admit such lack. "I cannot expect more than I am."

Mrs. Medora waved a hand as if swatting at gnats. "That's claptrap. Some women artists were from the slums of Paris. Daughters of prostitutes. Children of factory workers. For centuries, critics and buyers ignored women's art, claiming subservience to male artists, but no longer. Names like Berthe Morisot, Mary Cassatt, and Marie Bracquemond have championed women's Impressionism. Degas even invited Mary Cassatt to exhibit her work with male Impressionists."

Colleen's heart sped up at hearing the hope Mrs. Medora poured out through her story. She knew of Degas and his work. "Really? That's amazing."

Mr. Alson's wife chuckled, her eyes dancing. "It is. Moreover, Mary Cassatt had long fought for women's equality, the right to vote—and to have art scholarships for women." She stood and pulled a sheet of paper from her pocket. "I happen to have an application for such a scholarship here, which Mr. Alson and I would like you to fill out. We will personally send it to the committee for approval."

Colleen's jaw fell open, but she snapped it closed. As her heart took flight, her breath came in tiny puffs. Was the woman taunting her, teasing her? Could such an impossible, miraculous gift come to one such as her? She must be dreaming.

And on today, of all days—her twentieth birthday. At that moment, hope soared on the breeze. Could such a thing possibly come true?

Mrs. Medora handed her the paper, but Colleen couldn't read it for the tears in her eyes. "Thank you, ma'am, but I don't deserve this. I couldn't possibly stand before such an august group of people. I'm simply a laundry lass who likes to draw."

From around the corner, Mr. Alson appeared and joined them on the porch. "Miss Sullivan, we don't offer such a gift to just anyone. You are only the second in my entire career to whom I've extended such an opportunity. Take it. Who knows if they will select you, but if you don't try, you'll never know."

Colleen stood and curtsied low. "Sir. Ma'am. Thank you for honoring me with this. I would like to try, but I have no samples of my work. They are all gone."

Mr. Alson's brow furrowed. "All the beautiful drawings I saw? Gone? Where? How?"

How could she answer that without lying? Without putting herself in danger with Marshall? "They're at the bottom of the river, sir. An... accident."

Colleen heard a click of a tongue and glanced behind her. There, behind the screen door leading to the utility room, stood Marshall.

Scowling.

Watching the entire exchange.

~ ~ ~

Jack whistled a sea shanty tune. Providence smiled on him. Being sent to the bay for supplies allowed him to spend a fair bit of his hard-earned money on much-needed items.

He hurried to Comfort cottage carrying a large basket, a linen napkin hiding a green bottle, two glasses, and a sizable package wrapped in brown paper and string. His mouth twitched, a hopeful grin turning his lips up, excitement building with each step he took. Would his surprise tickle her?

In exactly the same place he'd seen her hours earlier, Colleen sat on the porch, still mending. Hard at work. The woman was relentless, faithful, patient. How she completed such mundane every day was a mystery to him. He'd go stark-raving mad.

Jack stepped onto the porch. "May I join you for a little refreshment?"

Colleen blinked, her gaze snapping toward the utility room. Had her pretty face turned ashen in the moment? "Let's walk. I need to stretch my legs."

She set down a pair of white captain's trousers and followed him down the steps.

They walked in comfortable silence until they came to their usual spot overlooking the main channel. A large freighter saluted, blowing the low, long ship's whistle three times. Several sailors waved, and they waved back.

Colleen broke the silence. "Any news of the troubles in Europe?"

Jack frowned, his heart sinking into a sullen pit of sadness in an instant. He wanted this to be a happy moment, not one with terrible talk of war. "Just yesterday, August 10, Austria and Hungary joined forces and invaded Russia."

Colleen's eyes misted with a mixture of confusion, apprehension, and trepidation. "Mighty Russia? Oh, no! Then it truly is becoming a world war."

He agreed, a twinge of sorrow tainting his tone. "I fear it is, and I've not heard from my family."

She patted his hand. "The post is slow. There's hardly been time for a letter to cross the ocean, even without war. Have faith, my friend."

She squared her shoulders and lifted her chin as if to bolster him with both her words and her posture. A habit that he'd come to love.

Jack swallowed his concerns. For now. "Shall we turn to happier topics? I have a surprise for you."

He pulled out the bottle and presented it to her, imitating the sommelier he had seen in the fancy Viennese restaurant his *opa* took him to before he emigrated.

She giggled. "I don't drink wine, sir. Never tasted it, and I certainly would not while I'm working." She glanced back toward the cottage, a flicker of fear crossing her chocolate-fondue eyes. "Mrs. Marshall has eyes in the back of her head, that one."

He waved a hand to dispel her concern. "You're safe with me, my fair *fraulein*. It's not alcohol. It's a brand-new drink. Ginger ale. I think you'll find it rather refreshing."

Colleen's brows furrowed, but she smiled with an air of curiosity. She licked her full, red lips. "What a treat. Thank you for thinking of me. Especially today. I must tell you about my conversation with Mrs. Medora."

Jack studied her face. Soft. Gentle. Eager. He'd wait and hear her tale before he served the drink.

Colleen fairly exploded with excitement as she conveyed the meeting with Mr. Alson and his wife. Yet her eyes were a prison of secrets that refused to divulge deeper concerns. Her fears. Such a complex tangle of womanhood. She seemed thrilled yet exasperated. Determined but unsure. How could he reconcile the jumbled amalgamation of who she was?

She appraised him with a touch of offense. "Are you listening, Jack?"

His face flamed, and he clenched his jaw, making the small tick near his eye twitch fiercely. "Sorry. I was distracted. What did you say?"

"I can't do it, Jack. I have no art to submit as samples of my work." Her voice quivered as if she would cry. "Marshall destroyed them."

Jack took her right hand and stroked the now-scarred back with his thumb. "I still have the Indian sketch, and you can make more. I've seen how quickly you work. How beautifully you create your masterpieces. You can do it again. Even better."

Colleen sniffed. "I need paper. Pencils. Supplies. But I can't afford them. I'll soon finish working here, so I must save my money to hold me over until I can find other work."

Jack slipped the package from his basket and handed it to her. His lips quivered as he held back a grin. "For you."

Colleen raised an eyebrow, a corner of her lips turning up with it. A trace of sadness flew away like dandelion seeds. "How did you know today was my birthday?"

Jack guffawed. For several moments, he could barely contain himself. Wasn't it just like God to guide him on such an occasion? "I didn't know. But happy birthday, Colleen."

He held out the package until, after several long moments, she took it. The ginger ale could wait.

Slowly, painstakingly, Colleen untied the string and unfolded the brown paper. The wooden box was unmarked, but when she creaked it open, she gasped. One large tear dropped onto the palate of watercolor paints he'd bought for her. Beside the palate lay three different size brushes.

Colleen stared at the gift, then she surveyed his face. Back and forth she looked at the paints and then at him. She held her hands to her chest and didn't touch the present, as if she couldn't believe they were real.

Jack chuckled, his heart racing like a steamer on the high seas. "Look underneath."

Her eyes grew wide and her mouth formed a pretty 'O', even so, she didn't touch the gift. Instead, he reached over, picked up box with the watercolors and brushes to reveal a professional artist's sketchpad underneath.

"Gracious. Have I died and gone to heaven?" A small giggle slipped from her lips that grew into a full-blown laugh. Before long, her mirth traveled up to her eyes. "Really? Really and truly?"

Jack acknowledged her with a grin so wide it pulled on his dry lips. "Happy birthday. May this be the beginning of dreams coming true."

Colleen's laugh turned into tears of joy. She leaned against him, leaned her head on his shoulder. "Thank you. I've never, ever received a birthday present before."

His heart clamped tight, and for a moment, her confession caused his throat to thicken. But then, Jack began singing the simple tune that had become famous just two years ago. "Happy birthday to you. Happy birthday to you. Happy birthday, dear Colleen. Happy birthday to you."

She sniffled for several minutes, wiping her eyes and nose on a handkerchief she pulled from her pocket. Finally, she whispered. "This has been the best day of my life. Truly."

Jack gently sat her up and pulled out the green bottle. "There's more to come. Shall we?"

Colleen consented, her eyes tinged with red but the tears gone. "What's it called again?"

"Ginger ale."

He poured two glasses, and they clinked them together like royalty at a ball, laughing at the joy of it. It pleased him to make this woman smile.

Colleen smelled the spicy drink and giggled. "It has bubbles."

Jack chuckled. "And it tastes good." He took a big gulp, not realizing the fizz would catch in his nose. He sputtered and choked, trying to stop the tickle. He laughed, his face burning with embarrassment.

Dummkoph.

"Sip it slowly, *Fraulein.*"

Her face lit up. "I will."

At her sincere response, his breath caught in his chest.

Might he one day hear a similar response in a markedly different situation?

~ ~ ~

Colleen slipped off her apron as the sun set in the west, and she shared the tales of the day with her roommate. A day she'd never forget.

Tara let down her hair and brushed the long tresses. "I'm so happy for you, Colleen. That's crackin'. Just think, if you had never come here, you'd never would have had this opportunity."

One loud rap, followed by the door swinging wide open, disrupted their conversation. Marshall. Her eyes full of vehemence.

On the warpath.

"Colleen. Come with me. Now."

She jerked her by the arm and fairly dragged her out of the room, slamming the door behind her. "What's the meaning of your secrecy and deceit?"

What was she talking about? Colleen felt as if the woman punched her in the gut. "Ma'am?"

Marshall's wicked glare burned into her soul, and Colleen shrank against the wall. "You're a sniveling, sneaky *orphan*? Information you dishonestly hid from me. You have no business serving the likes of the Clarks."

The ogre shoved her against the wall. Her head slammed against the wood. Hard.

"You must go."

CHAPTER 11

Colleen sat at the kitchen table, the kerosene lamp casting eerie shadows on the walls. Several flies buzzed near the screened windows, and outside, bullfrogs croaked to one another. Other than that, the cottage was quiet.

Her stout-waisted aunt poured tea into a plain ceramic pot and waddled to the table. Her triple chins wobbled like half-set jam, her face wrinkled with the cares of the world. Indeed, her features betrayed her stern, steely personality.

Yet Colleen was grateful for her, though she'd only known the woman existed since the previous winter. The orphanage somehow tracked down her aunt and contacted her in Chicago. Aunt Gertie was the only kin she had ever known, and the woman mercifully and clandestinely secured her the position she now held. At the moment.

Colleen and her aunt kept their kinship shrouded in secrecy all these months, sneaking quick chats here and there, whispering concerns and warnings when no one was around. Early morning visits and late-night prattle, surreptitiously getting acquainted, albeit through her aunt's veil of austerity. When others were present, she and her aunt alleged there was no connection between them apart from serving the Clark family on Comfort Island.

Aunt Gertie poured them both cups of tea, slipping a butter cookie onto each of their saucers. Steam from the tea curled in little circles, dissipating into the evening darkness.

Auntie slurped her tea loudly and grumbled, staring at Colleen under thick brows. "What now?"

Colleen's confession bunched into a ball at the bottom of her throat. She swallowed it. "Mrs. Marshall knows."

Aunt Gertie scowled, her eyes growing wide and her face flushing a deep, strawberry red. Sweat beaded on her forehead, and she swiped it away with her shirtsleeve. "Knows what?"

"That I'm an orphan." Colleen's voice cracked. "I don't know how she found out."

Aunt Gertie rocked back and forth, the rhythm of her foot tapping the floor keeping pace with Colleen's racing heart. "Oh dear. I should have disclosed the information to Mrs. Lacey. I'm sure she wouldn't mind. Now keeping it secret, we may both be in hot water."

Rock. Tap. Rock Tap.

Colleen sipped her tea, looking for an answer to the dilemma. "I'm sorry I put you at risk, Aunt Gertie. I should've stayed away."

The woman froze. "How did she find out? Who did you tell?"

Colleen shrugged. "Tara guessed after I cried out in the night."

"I'll tan the girl's hide." Aunt Gertie griped, resuming her nervous toe-tapping twitch. "She'll be out on her ear."

"I'm sure she didn't betray me. She's a friend, a good person." Colleen's voice rose with her emotions. "Blame me."

Aunt Gertie slapped the table, and the commotion splashing tea into the saucers. "It's Marshall. She's the insidious one, but I still don't understand the power she has over everyone. She doesn't know about your failed engagement, does she? About his death?"

Like a smack in the face, her aunt's words pained her. She'd tried to forget the matter, though she prayed for Peter's soul and the souls of all those who perished on *The Empress of Ireland* that fateful night. But she didn't know him, and that was that. Still, if Marshall knew...

Colleen shook her head, her hands sweating about what might happen if the ogre knew. "I've not told a soul."

Aunt Gertie rolled her eyes, wiping her sweaty brow again. "Good. And keep it that way. One secret is enough. Two is two too many."

She had to confess that her third secret was already out. "She knows I'm Irish. She called me a mick."

Aunt Gertie shrugged, puffing an exasperated breath. "That's not a big deal these days. Don't worry about that."

Colleen's hands trembled, and so did her lower lip. "The nuns cared. Punished us for being Irish. Called us micks and bog-trotters and prods, but I never knew what those names meant. I still don't."

Her head pounded like it always had after she endured the regular orphanage castigations. Hopelessness clamped Colleen's heart tighter and tighter. Would she never be free?

Her aunt broke into her thoughts. "We'll have to keep the woman's malevolent trap shut, that's what we'll do. Find some dirt and beat her at her own game. Get her dismissed before she causes any more trouble.

Let me think on it, but for now, stay out of her way and be off with you before she finds you not in bed."

"She's the one who hauled me from my room like I was a wayward dog." Colleen rose, set her teacup in the sink, and kissed her aunt on the cheek. "Thanks for the tea and for being my aunt."

Aunt Gertie gave a curt nod and turned to the sink. "Sleep well, niece."

Colleen left through the back door, stepping onto the moonlit porch. The faintest shuffle of feet sounded as she let out a silent gasp. Her breath caught in her throat, and she held it there, wishing she could magically disappear into the night.

Marshall clamped a hand over her mouth and seized her arm, yanking her down the steps and into the forested darkness beyond earshot of anyone. "Why are you still out of your bed? Am I a nursemaid to foundlings, ragamuffins, and waifs? Or to an underhanded liar who has an aunt as her accomplice? Black mourning clothes and seclusions should be your lot, not working for a well-to-do family." The woman shook her again, rattling her teeth and filling her eyes with stars. "I am an important employee of an honored and influential family. I have worked my way up to status and position, and I will not have the likes of a sniveling orphaned, widowed deceiver disrupt my rise to prominence. Not while I have breath." Marshall gave Colleen a small shove, throwing her off-balance. "Come morning, everyone will know your secrets. Mr. Alson won't be so fond of his little prodigy. Mrs. Clark will find you disgusting. Mrs. Medora will think you a scandal to be rid of. And your kraut, Jack? He'll throw you overboard and laugh you to scorn. You, miss, will be an abomination to anyone who has had the unfortunate experience of knowing you."

Then the ogre gave her another shove. A substantial push.

As if in slow motion, Colleen fell back, hitting the ground with a thump, her lungs expelling air in a quick, helpless puff. She tumbled in the sharp pine needles, then rolled down the bank, feeling like she'd never breath again. Gasping. Flailing. Trying to catch hold of something. Anything—until something caught her.

Then everything went dark.

~ ~ ~

Colleen opened her eyes to the dew-heavy morning filtering the summer sunshine through the trees. Where was she? What had happened?

She shivered, rubbing her arms to ward off the chill. Her head ached, and when she put her hand to her crown, a large goose egg felt sticky. Bloody.

She tried to sit up, but she felt dizzy, nauseous. Her ribs hurt, and she could barely take enough breath to move.

"Miss Sullivan? What in heaven's name happened to you?" Mr. Alson appeared just above her head, dropping his fishing pole just inches from her. "Steady, lass. I'm here. You're safe now."

Colleen blinked back the blur of his face and tried to sit up, but Mr. Alson stopped her. He gently lifted her head. Gentle fingers probed her hair, locating the bloody bump. He took off his jacket and formed a pillow for her. "I need to get help. Will you be all right for a few more minutes?"

Her mouth felt like cotton filled it, and when she tried to speak, the words failed to form. She dipped her chin, but that made her head swim. She closed her eyes and exhaled, biting the inside of her cheek at the pinch of pain in her abdomen.

Mr. Alson touched her shoulder. "Don't move. I'll be right back."

Truth was, she couldn't move else she'd vomit. She tried to remember what happened, but the last thing she recalled was a dream of falling down a steep precipice. Wait! Was it a dream—or was it real? She slowly turned her head. There. The hill.

It *was* real.

But what had happened?

Her mind, a muddled mess, searched her memory. Aunt Gertie. Tea. Talk. Marshall.

The ogre had heard her talking to her aunt. She knew everything!

And she had pushed her.

"Ugh…"

Colleen squeezed her eyes shut at the horror of the truth. The very last person in her world who should know her secrets had found her out. Now, they would all know her shame, her deceit, her lack of character.

Mr. Alson. Her hope for a future. Gone.

Jack. Would he verbalize his revulsion when he knew her past? Knew who she really was? Or would he simply turn his back and walk away?

At that moment, she wished the ground would swallow her whole. Or the river would sweep her away.

Forever.

~ ~ ~

Jack took the empty seat next to Tara at the servants' table. "Good morning, *Fraulein*. Where's Colleen?"

The young maid's eyes darted back and forth as if looking for a ghost to appear at any moment. Her brow furrowed, and a small moan escaped her lips.

She leaned over, keeping her voice low. ""I... I don't know. I don't know what to do. She didn't come to bed last night. *All* night."

Jack's pulse pounded in his temples. Did Colleen flee from Mrs. Marshall's wickedness without saying goodbye? Even to Tara? Surely not. Did Marshall have her work through the night? Possible, but improbable. Was she hurt? Or trapped somewhere?

"I'll find out." He jumped up from the table and hurried out the back door, almost bumping into Mr. Alson. "Sorry, sir. I was just…"

Mr. Alson grabbed him, his face etched with fear. "Come and help me, man. She's hurt. I think badly."

Jack sucked in a horrified breath. "Who, sir? Who's injured?"

"Miss Sullivan."

"Dear God, no!" Jack swallowed the bile rising in his throat and offered the only prayer he could think of. "Help, Lord."

He followed Mr. Alson as they scurried through the trees, over the hill, and down to the river. There, lying by the water's edge, Colleen turned her head, pain written all over her face. Then she closed her eyes and turned away.

Enough was enough. No more keeping secrets. No more hiding the truth of Marshall's wickedness. Fire surged through his veins as the twitch near his eye jolted to life. He caught Mr. Alson's arm. "Sir, I fear this was Mrs. Marshall's doing."

Mr. Alson stopped and tilted his head. "The maid? What are you talking about, man?"

Jack lowered his voice. Marshall wouldn't thank Mr. Alson for referring to her as hired help. The woman thought far too highly of herself. And Colleen would be in no mood to hear his disclosure, even though her superior deserved it—and more. "She's a cruel taskmaster, and her anger is out of control. She's pushed Colleen before. She seems to have some sort of vendetta or hatred against Colleen. I saw it with my own eyes."

Mr. Alson gawked at Colleen. "We'll discuss this later. For now, let's take care of Miss Sullivan."

When they reached her, Colleen was struggling to get up. She was also shivering. Jack slipped off his flannel work shirt and draped it over her, tucking it around her as if to swaddle her. "You're going to be all right, *Fraulein*. You're safe now."

Colleen's eyes fluttered as if fighting sleep, but Jack bent over her and patted her cheek gently. "Stay with us, Colleen. Stay awake. You'll be fine."

Her lips quivered, her breath coming in little puffs. She didn't open her eyes, but her grimace screamed she was in pain.

"Hello down there!" Cook shouted from the hilltop above them. Tara—and Marshall—stood there, too. "Is she all right?"

Mr. Alson extended his palm toward them. "Stay where you are. We will take care of her. You—young maid—please fetch us a blanket and towels. Cook, gather bandages and be ready when we bring her to the cottage. Mrs. Marshall, alert Captain Comstock to ready the steamer to transport the injured girl to the bay."

The three women disappeared from sight, and Mr. Alson put an index finger to his lips. Then he made a slicing motion across his neck.

Jack understood.

Say nothing.

For now.

~ ~ ~

Jack paced the medical clinic porch, glancing at Mr. Alson and Mrs. Marshall, who sat in wicker chairs awaiting some news. Where was the sheriff the good doctor had summoned? And what could take Dr. Higgins so long?

If anything happened to Colleen, Mrs. Marshall would pay. He spewed out a breath and glared at the stone-faced woman. Even if Colleen recovered, Mrs. Marshall would still pay.

Patience. Time and patience would make things right.

Hopefully.

After more than an hour, Dr. Higgins stepped onto the porch, his face grim. He leaned against the porch railing, facing Mr. Alson and Mrs. Marshall. "The woman has suffered a concussion, a head wound, and a cracked rib. It's a miracle the rib didn't puncture her lung and kill her. I stitched up the gash on her head and wrapped her ribs, but she'll need time and rest to recover fully. How did this happen? Do you know?"

Jack stepped up to answer, facing Mr. Alson and Mrs. Marshall. "I can guess what happened. Mrs. Marshall, would you care to give a first-hand accounting of last night's events?"

Mrs. Marshall's eyes narrowed as she almost growled her reply. "What are you implying, sir?"

Jack folded his arms over his chest to keep from punching her. "I am implying, madam, that she suffered these injuries because you pushed her down the hill. That *you* caused this accident."

Mrs. Marshall cackled like a menacing crow. "I've never heard anything so preposterous in all my life. I've been nothing but a good supervisor to her. How dare you!"

His fists balled tight, but he willed them to his sides. "That is a lie. I've heard you berate her with the wickedness of a saloon operator. Weeks ago, I saw you shove her near the laundry. And on the back porch. And slap her face. More than once. And what about the burn on her hand? Hmm? I suspect you had something to do with that, too."

Marshall's facade melted before their eyes. Her eyes snapped furiously from Jack to Mr. Alson to Dr. Higgins like a trapped feral cat before a pack of wild dogs.

When she finally spoke, her voice was an octave higher. "Miss Sullivan is a deceitful scamp who all should judge and found wanting. I have proof this pretty little wench is not who she claims to be."

With the audacity of a lunatic, Marshall slipped two letters from her pocket and waved them in the air, glaring at Jack. "Here is a letter from her *fiancé's* mother claiming he is dead. And here is a note from her *Aunt* Gertrude—*your* cook, Mr. Alson—who never disclosed that the no-good *orphan* was her niece. She, too, should be out on the street."

Marshall's triumphant grin spewed vitriol. "Miss Sullivan is an Irish foundling, a waif, an orphan who has deceived all of us with her pretty little face to get a position under your roof. To weasel her way into your good graces, for who knows what evil intent? Perhaps to poison your food or slit your throat while you sleep? Beware, sir, of such a reprobate. You should cast her far from you fine folk."

Jack stood his ground, keeping his voice steady, his gaze strong. "You didn't answer my question, Mrs. Marshall. Did you push Miss Sullivan down the hill last night and leave her there to die?"

Dr. Higgins and Mr. Alson joined Jack, one on either side, the three forming a barricade against Marshall. Dr. Higgins pulled a pad from his pocket and read. "According to the patient, you, Mrs. Marshall, accosted her on the back porch, covering her mouth and…"

Mrs. Marshall popped out of her chair and interrupted his declaration. She turned to Mr. Alson, wringing her hands together. "I was only protecting you and your mother, Mr. Clark, as I should. You do not know what trouble this waif has been under my care."

Mr. Alson stepped forward. "Silence. Let us be done with the matter."

The door to the clinic opened, and the bear-like, barrel-chested Sheriff Wilson stepped out. "Mrs. Alice

Smith Marshall, you are under arrest for assault and battery of Miss Colleen Sullivan—and the attempted murder of your younger sister, Annabelle, four years ago while in your care. Neither of these young women deserved what you have inflicted upon either of them."

Mrs. Marshall let out an ear-piercing scream and tried to sidestep the sheriff, but Jack grabbed her and held tight. A satisfied snicker slipped from his lips as the sheriff handcuffed her and led her away.

~ ~ ~

Colleen sucked in shallow breaths as she lay in the silence of the doctor's clinic, the tic-toc of a clock the only sound. She ached all over. Especially her chest and head. And her heart. By now, everyone must know her shame.

She'd go west. Reinvent herself. Perhaps paint scenes of Indians and cowboys on the wild frontier.

But she didn't want to leave. She wanted to be here. With Jack. With her aunt. With her dream.

An unearthly scream broke the silence, followed immediately by a second. It didn't sound quite human. Maybe a cat run over by a wagon? The shuffling of many feet on a wooden floor sounded like a scuffle outside. A woman's voice, raised, shouting words she couldn't quite make out. More footsteps. Then everything quieted down.

She flinched at a gentle knock on the door. "Come in."

Jack stepped into the room and smiled. She searched the deep, dark pools of his eyes, looking for disgust and loathing. Instead, something else marred his usually jovial expression. Worry, concern—perhaps even care? He pulled up a chair and sat, taking her hand but saying nothing. He simply stroked it over and over, drawing a finger over her scars with a gentleness of a feather. She closed her eyes, praying for him to be kind while he said goodbye.

Finally, after what felt like an eternity, he spoke, almost in a whisper. "I knew you had secrets. Knew your heart was a deep well of mystery, of pain. I longed for you to tell me those secrets, to unburden your hurts to someone—someone who cares. But you never did."

No matter how hard Colleen tried to hold back the dam, tears leaked from her still-closed eyes, ran down her cheeks, and pooled in her ears. But she kept her eyes closed, didn't move. Didn't respond.

He'd found her wanting, just like everyone did.

If only he'd leave.

And let her be.

Alone with her shame.

CHAPTER 12

Trapped. That's how Colleen felt. Too dizzy to move her head in inch. And with every breath she took, sharp pain exploded in her chest, like someone was ripping her apart. Was she dying?

Jack just sat there in silence, judging her. The secretive, broken orphan that she was. He must despise her, and she wished she'd die. Disappear. Never to be seen again.

Her reputation, what she had of it, was now ruined forever. Her employment likely terminated. And worst of all, her relationship with Jack and Tara—and with

Mr. Alson and Mrs. Medora—would never be the same. Perhaps Aunt Gertie would disown her, too.

She'd be alone again. Like always.

She might as well be dead.

Colleen kept her eyes closed. Pretended to sleep. She couldn't face the man who sat beside her, still holding her hand. Perhaps after a while he'd leave her be. To sleep. To die.

Another knock. Why wouldn't everyone just pretend she didn't exist?

Mr. Alson's voice, barely above a whisper. "Sheriff wants a word, Jack. I'll sit with her."

Colleen squeezed her eyes tight and sucked in a breath, sending a bullet through her chest. She slowly, carefully exhaled to ease the pain. If she pretended to sleep, maybe Mr. Alson wouldn't speak to her, wouldn't reprimand and then dismiss her—yet.

But pretending didn't work. Mr. Alson gently patted her hand. When she didn't respond, he touched her shoulder. Finally, Colleen opened her eyes and blinked, pasting her lips tight together, refusing to open a discussion that, she was sure, wouldn't end well.

Mr. Alson smiled, his eyes soft. "Glad you're awake. In much pain?"

Colleen warmed at his gentle tone. "A little."

"The doctor says otherwise. I'm sorry." Mr. Alson's voice rang with concern. "Sorry for what you've suffered. I regret we didn't know what Marshall was doing to you. But she is now in the sheriff's custody, charged with assault and battery. There is more. The sheriff informed us that the evil woman is from Toronto, and they've been looking for her. After maiming and almost killing her younger sister in a furious rage, Marshall left her for dead and fled the country, reinventing herself and finding employment with us. She hoodwinked her way into our good graces. We didn't know her past, or we would never have hired her."

Colleen's brow furrowed, and even that small movement hurt. She licked dry lips. "But all she said is true, sir. I am Irish. I am an orphan. My fiancé died in May, and I should be in mourning."

Mr. Alson chuckled, but his amusement didn't reach his eyes. Instead, they shone with care. "My dear, none of that matters. It's not where you come from that constitutes worth, but what's in your heart."

Colleen blinked. "That's what my roommate, Tara, said."

"She's a clever girl. We like smart women in our employ." Mr. Alson sighed. "I can't say I'm pleased that you and Cook failed to disclose everything when you applied for the position, but none of that is of consequence. What Mrs. Marshall did is."

Colleen turned her head, and the room spun. She closed her eyes and swallowed the bile trying to slip up her throat. Once the nausea passed, she addressed the artist, her employer. "Please, sir, don't sack Cook and make her pay for my inadequacies. She meant only good. I was about to be cast out of the orphanage to live on the streets, and she had compassion. She wasn't trying to be insubordinate."

Mr. Alson took her hand and patted it. "I know. Fear not, Miss Sullivan." He paused and leaned over to look her directly in the face. "May I call you Colleen, since we're fellow artists—and friends?"

Colleen swallowed. "Sir? Of course, sir."

He grew somber, and for a long while said nothing. Finally, when he spoke, his tone was casual and friendly, like when they painted side by side. "I want you to listen carefully, Colleen. Your aunt is not in danger of losing her position. Neither are you. I will take care of your expenses while you heal, and my family will continue your salary."

Colleen's mind swirled with the information. Was she dreaming? She tried to understand. To comprehend what Mr. Alson was saying, but it sounded like a dream. She pressed her eyes shut, concentrating on his words and what it all meant.

He spoke again, gently squeezing her hand. "But, my dear, talented girl. You have some decisions to make. You are on the precipice. You can choose to live in the shadows of your past pain and hurts. You can continue to believe the lies of who others say you are. Or you can let go of the prison they have put you in and be free to become all who God has planned for you to be. It's your choice, Colleen, and only you can make it."

Mr. Alson grew quiet, but he didn't leave. He sat there as if he was waiting for her to absorb the information and decide then and there.

She whispered into the air, refusing to open her eyes. "How can I choose something different from who I am?"

The chair creaked as he shifted in his seat. "Your past doesn't have to define you. You can use it for a purpose—you can paint the scars, remember?"

Colleen thought back on that magical day when she felt so inspired, whole—alive—as she painted that German village. Her mind soared and her fingers flew as she allowed them to be free. She chose. In those moments, her past or the terrible things others said about her, did to her, hadn't defined her. She simply took the pain and used them to paint.

She painted the scars.

"I… I think I understand, sir, and I want to be free. Truly."

Her voice cracked, and more tears slipped from the corners of her eyes. Her chest heaved, but it hurt so badly she willed herself to lie still.

Mr. Alson slipped her hand to his lips and kissed it, not romantically, but in an affirming, fatherly way. The touch warmed her from her hand to her aching head. "Take all the time you need to heal—inside and out. Then, when you're ready, you have work to do. Art to produce. An application to fill out."

He still wanted to help her? Still believed in her?

Colleen opened her eyes and waited for the room to stop swimming. She slowly turned her head to look at him, a twinkle in his eyes.

"Thank you, Mr. Alson. I will."

He chuckled. "Good. Then I've done my work here. You rest and get well."

He stood, bent over her bed, and kissed her on the forehead. Then he left the room without another word.

Would she choose?

Could she finally be free?

Yes!

~ ~ ~

Jack heaved a sigh of relief when Colleen ambled into the servants' dining room. It had been almost three weeks—over a week before she returned to the island after recuperating at the doctor's office and almost two more confined to her room quietly healing. Since she stayed in her room, he'd not seen her or talked with her. Instead, he wrote letters. Paragraphs that opened parts of him he didn't know were closed. Words that spoke of their future and hope and promises of better days.

And fears as well. In that terrible month of August, Germany had declared war on Russia, France, and Belgium. In turn, Britain and Japan declared war on Germany, pulling Canada into the conflict.

While Colleen healed, Europe was splitting apart, but America remained neutral. So where did he fit into this jumbled puzzle of hatred and war? Should he fight for his homeland or stay and find a new life here? He prayed for peace, but it hadn't come. Pleaded for direction, but the heavens seemed silent.

Colleen's letters to him begged him to stay. To have faith that his family was safe. To wait for their missive. She gave him just enough strength to find patience day after day.

Now here she was, her beautiful smile responding to cheers and welcomes from the staff. Finally... they could talk again face to face.

Jack slipped into the empty chair next to her. "Welcome back. It's so good to see you again."

Colleen giggled, pouring cream into her coffee. "It's good to be back."

Tara waved from across the table. "Aye, it's a crackin' day for all of us."

The butler tapped his butter knife on his glass, calling the staff to silence. Mrs. Lacey stood by his side, her usual sweet smile warming the way. "Attention, all. Mrs. Lacey and I would like to welcome Colleen back and let you know that, starting today, she will assume Mrs. Marshall's position as housemaid. Mrs. Lacey will train her while she continues to mend, and Colleen will return to Chicago with us after we close up the cottage next week."

Colleen's mouth dropped open, her eyes wide and her face growing pale. Had she not known about this promotion? Did she even want it?

The staff clapped as one, and Mrs. Lacey held up a hand. "We will continue to use the local washerwoman for the laundry until we return to Chicago."

Breakfast continued, but surprise quenched Jack's appetite. He leaned over and whispered, "Did you know about this?"

Colleen ducked her chin. "Not a clue." She chanced a glimpse of Mrs. Lacey, who grinned broadly and acknowledged her.

Colleen nodded back. "That's that, I guess."

Apparently, she'd accept the job. But what about him? The Clarks hired him as the Comfort Island groundskeeper. That didn't include an invitation to Chicago. Perhaps it was a sign that he should go to war.

And fight for his homeland.

But did he belong there?

Or here?

~ ~ ~

Did she hear right? A housemaid for the Clarks? Colleen had never dreamed of such a position, nor had they said anything about it. Not Aunt Gertie. Not Mrs. Lacey. Not anyone.

Yet the news thrilled her. No matter how hard the work, she'd make them all proud. If she had to work from dawn till dusk, she'd excel.

She'd choose. Choose to be all God wanted her to be, whether she became the best housemaid the Clarks ever had—or whatever God had for her future. Perhaps a housemaid was her calling? Perhaps not.

But what about Jack? He was the looming question in her world. Would he go to war? Would he stay? And if he did, would he follow her to Chicago? For now, she would put Jack in the hands of the only One who held the answers.

After a full day of Mrs. Lacey's patient training, Colleen ached to finally spend time with Jack, to show him her art before she handed it to the Clarks to be submitted to the scholarship committee.

She held her portfolio in her hands, remembering the special moments of the past few weeks. Memories she'd treasure forever.

While she convalesced, Colleen had completed the seventeen pieces of art she now held in her hands. Mr. Alson and Mrs. Medora helped her choose twelve to send with her scholarship application—six pencil sketches and six watercolors that she created, thanks to Jack's extravagant gift. She giggled at the realization that her confinement wasn't just for healing alone. In it, the Clarks had prodded her on to try for the art training scholarship.

What's more, Mr. Alson insisted she use the empty, third-floor copula room as a studio. "The natural light will help you excel," he'd said. Her time of healing was for more than just her body's care. Her mind, her heart, her emotions healed, too.

The day after Mr. Alson set her to work in the copula, he took a break from coaching her to descend the narrow staircase while she worked with watercolors. She thought he was leaving, but he stopped and sketched on the stairway wall.

He chuckled. He laughed. He even guffawed once, and she wondered what he was doing. His compositions were always serious, poignant, masterful.

When he finished, he asked her to come and see it. "It's time for you to critique my work, Colleen. I've been picking apart yours all day, so now it's your turn."

Colleen put down her brush and stepped into the stairwell. The artist's grin held back a chuckle that danced in his eyes. "What do you think?"

He tried to be serious but failed miserably. Still, Colleen played along, pasting on a furrowed brow and demeanor she imagined might match the most professional art critic. "Well, the Thousand Islands Yacht Club is a fine likeness, I must say. The boat you named I.O.U., however, needs a little more detail. But sir, I think your cartoon depiction of the captain is the perfect likeness of Captain Comstock, especially in the eyes."

Mr. Alson burst into peals of laughter, and Colleen did, too. The artist's cartoon was nothing like she'd ever seen in his work, and it both baffled and delighted her.

After wiping tears from his eyes, Mr. Alson shrugged. "I just wanted to make you laugh, my dear. Nothing more."

"Thank you, sir. You succeeded."

Colleen carefully curtsied where she stood on a narrow step. He deserved it.

During the following weeks, Mr. Alson and his wife visited her often, meeting with her in the copula, commending her on each piece she completed. He challenged her to adjust this or that, and once to start over and try again. He offered advice. Counsel. Wisdom. And she appreciated every tidbit of training and employed the various techniques he showed her as best she could.

And she grew. Grew in her craft. Grew in self-confidence. Grew in healing a heart and body that desperately needed it.

Most of all, she learned the power of choosing God's best.

Colleen hugged her portfolio as she stepped off the back porch and made her way to her favorite spot on the river. She just knew Jack would be there.

As she hoped, he sat where they first met, on the rock outcropping overlooking the main channel. She'd miss the beauty of this place, the magic of its mystery. Soon she'd be traveling to a place she'd never seen, to a future she could only imagine.

"Good evening, Jack."

Jack scooted to his feet and smiled, but his eyes held a melancholy that alarmed her. Had he decided to return to Austria? To fight in the war?

He observed her portfolio, and his face brightened. "You brought them? I was wondering if I'd ever see them."

In three paces he was at her side, offering his elbow as if escorting her onto the dance floor of an elegant ballroom. She took it, and they ambled to their special spot and sat.

Her heart thumped as she opened her book. "The top twelve are for the scholarship application. The Clarks helped me choose them."

Would Jack like them, too? She held her breath. His opinion was so important to her.

He slowly flipped through all the pieces without saying a word. Then he turned back to the first one. "I'm astounded at the leap you've taken in your artistry. Truly."

Colleen shrugged. "Mr. Alson is a wonderful teacher. He's revealed techniques and skills I didn't know existed."

Jack studied the first watercolor, a scene of a beach with a dog scampering in the water, chasing a gaggle of geese. He chuckled. "I can hear Champ bark and the geese honk in fear. Splendid, my dear."

She gleamed, touching the painting. "I couldn't have done it without your gift. Thank you."

He nodded, turning the page to a sunset scene blazing with color. He tapped the picture. "Best investment I've ever made, I assure you."

Page after page, he smiled and commented and affirmed her work. One by one, her heart swelled with joy. With hope.

With love.

When he finished, he reverently closed the portfolio and set it aside. "Thank you for sharing this with me. Seeing it, experiencing it, is a gift. They are beautiful. You, Colleen, are beautiful."

He reached around her shoulders and pulled her to him, giving her a tender squeeze. Then he kissed the top of her head.

Her heart wanted to soar, but she reined it in with an invisible leash strong enough to hold an ox. She wouldn't fall prey to flattery. When Sister Bertha flattered her, not far behind would be the sting of bad news or an accusation, whether or not true, and usually a paddle. Sister Bertha loved her paddle.

Jack repeated his proclamation. "You are, Colleen, oh so exquisite."

The old Colleen couldn't believe such words. The new woman craved them. Her thoughts warred within her.

She chose the new. "Thank you, Jack."

Jack held her close as they watched the setting sun shimmering with the colors of the rainbow. Vibrant.

Strong. True. Tomorrow would have cares of its own—of war, of peace, of goodbyes, of the unknown.

But now?

She chose now.

CHAPTER 13

Colleen meandered along the shore, her thoughts a mixture of joy and sadness. She was leaving this island a different woman from when she came. She'd been a broken, shame-filled orphan, but here she'd chosen freedom—to dream, to sketch, to live. Now she was on her way to healing and being filled with hope.

Comforted.

Yet she also knew she had more work to do before she could truly move forward, before she could be free. She loathed the choice, for it meant giving up the only thing she believed gave her strength. The only thing that had sustained her through the turmoil of life.

She had to forgive.

Forgive everyone. Let go of it all. All the hurts. All the pain. All the words meant to slash and wound.

The persecution. The prejudice. The punishments.

Only then could she be free. But how?

Colleen fell to her knees on the sandy beach, praying for God to help her. To ease the ache. To take away the memories. "Lord, I need You to show me how to let go. I choose to forgive all my past troubles. I want to leave it all behind, to never think about it again."

Paint the scars.

The words shot through her like a lightning bolt.

If she forgot the pain, she wouldn't be able to paint. Yet how could she remember without feeling the pain of those memories?

"Help me, Lord."

She observed the small rocks and pebbles scattered along the beach. Washed up during summer storms. If not for them, the beach would look perfect. A sharp-edged stone dug into her knee, so she removed it and tossed it in the river.

The irritation gone. The pain eradicated.

Colleen stood and collected more rocks and pebbles. When she had a handful, she studied them. Some were even pretty, sparkling with bits of shimmering mica. A picture she could paint.

She had a better idea. She tossed a stone in the river, heaving it far from her. "I forgive Sister Gregory." Then another. "I forgive Sister Bertha."

On and on she went—Sister Anthony. Sister Patricia. Everyone she could remember. Everyone who'd hurt her.

And her heart felt lighter. Freer.

But there was more to release—the weapons of cruelty.

The paddles, hands, sticks, rulers, belts.

The closets, cellars, outhouses, laundry rooms.

The words, names, accusations, lies, and threats.

The ogres. Hills.

Marshall. To her right, she spotted a rock the size of her head. Could she lift it? Could she heave it— Marshall—into the river? She must. She dug down into the sand, working her fingers into nooks and crannies in the rock. Bending at the knees, she gripped as though she'd never let go. Using her arms and back, she wiggled the rock in its nest. Then she drew a deep breath, exhaled, and lifted the granite piece.

With one big splash, she let go of it all. She chose to forgive.

Behind her, someone chuckled. The soft, deep sound startled her. Made her jump.

Jack. How long had he been there?

His puzzled brows rose over eyes filled with amusement. "I've been looking for you everywhere. What are you doing, my dear girl?"

Colleen giggled and shrugged, perspiration misting her brow. "Cleaning up the beach... and my heart."

She explained her epiphany, how she'd chosen to forgive.

Jack sucked in a breath, swept her into his arms, and kissed the top of her head. "You're the most amazing woman I've ever met, Colleen. I'd like to know every corner of who you are. Every aspect of such a strong, good woman. But right now, I have a surprise."

Colleen searched his handsome face. His dark eyes twinkled with secrets. He raised an eyebrow, a smile spreading across his face.

He took her hand and pulled her toward the cottage. "Come on. They're waiting."

Colleen let him lead her but questioned him as they climbed the hill. "Who is waiting? For what?"

Jack laughed, holding back from telling her anything. "You'll see. Patience, my sweet. But I know you'll like it."

Instead of taking her to the cottage, Jack led her down to the boathouse. Tara stood on the dock, biting the forefinger nail, her feet tippy-tapping in place as if dancing to music only she could hear. Captain Comstock waited there, too, next to the Clark's elegant steamer.

The captain tipped his hat. "Before you and Tara leave the beauty of this river, the Clarks would like to treat you to a ride on the *Mamie C* so you can fully experience the magic of the St. Lawrence. This way, miss."

Jack scooted close and whispered in her ear. "Told you I'd take you for a jaunt on the river. Sorry it took so long to happen."

Colleen chuckled. "Thank you, Jack."

As they took a seat on the boat, Tara giggled, slipping her arm into the crook of Colleen's elbow. "Isn't this wonderful? I've never been on the steamer nor gone through the narrows. Only to and from the bay in the skiff." She leaned in close to her ear and whispered. "I think this excursion might be to make amends for them being bamboozled by that wicked woman."

Colleen laughed, slipping a peek toward Jack. Dollars to donuts, he orchestrated this excursion. "Whatever the reason, let's enjoy ourselves."

Captain Comstock indicated Jack. "Mr. Weiss will serve as first mate for your voyage. I hope you find it delightful."

After tossing them an impish grin, the captain blew the steamer's whistle three times, sending misty white smoke from the valve on top of the boat's cabin.

Jack stood next to the captain and winked, pointing toward the skipper with his thumb. "He takes great pleasure in tooting his own horn."

They all laughed at Jack's quip, including Captain Comstock.

Once the steamer left the dock, the master mariner addressed them. "To get your river bearings, we'll first travel downriver toward the bay through the inside channel you've taken to get to the island. I believe you'll find it a smoother ride of a little more than a mile. On your right, or starboard, is New York State, to which Comfort Island and everything else you'll see today belong. But do you know that half of the eighteen hundred Thousand Islands belong to Canada?"

Colleen shuddered. Marshall was Canadian. Her ire rose, but she pushed it down.

I chose.

241

Captain Comstock steered *Mamie C*, pointing across the channel. "Canada is just beyond Wellesley Island, which is that large island to your left. The international boundary often weaves through the waters so that boaters may cross into Canada without even realizing it."

For a few minutes, they sailed in silence, Colleen enjoying the wind in her face and the surrounding beauty.

Jack broke the silence by pointing to their left. "We've just passed Stoney Crest, and we're now weaving between Wauwinel Islands and Cuba Island. Devil's Island is ahead of us, where they say a pirate named Bill Johnson hid from the British during the Patriot War."

Captain Comstock laughed. "Pure fabrication, son, but it's jolly fun local folklore."

For several more minutes, they sailed in silence, enjoying the views. Views Colleen seared into her memory to paint later.

Jack pointed at an island with two three-story homes. "We're now passing Cherry Island, home to the twin cottages owned by Straus and Abraham, the founders of Macy's Department store, and the beautiful red and white home called Casa Blanca."

He motioned toward Alexandria Bay, where Colleen had begun her journey to Comfort just months ago. "Ahead is the bay, but we're not stopping there today."

At the tip of Cherry Island, Captain Comstock veered the steamer to round the shore and slowed the steamer so they could get a good look at the impressive Casa Blanca.

Colleen wondered at the pretty white cottage with a red roof and the wide veranda with a plethora of white wicker furniture. Wouldn't it be grand to sit there and sip a glass of cool lemonade, watching the world go by?

Across the narrow river channel, she noticed a castle on a small island. "What's that, Jack?"

Jack followed her gaze and smiled. "It's Castle Rest, home of Mr. George Pullman of the Pullman railroad car fame."

Captain Comstock agreed. "In 1872, President Ulysses S. Grant visited the island, and that's how this area became so famous. People flocked to the Thousand Islands to build grand castles and mansions and summer homes."

Tara drew their attention back to Casa Blanca. She giggled and pointed at the huge stone lion and menacing gargoyles along the shore. "Those are dreadful, scary creatures."

Captain chuckled. "The gargoyles ward off evil spirits, but the mighty lion welcomes the island's visitors."

He eased the steamer into the main channel. "We're now in the narrows, a fifty-mile stretch of river that is formidable to navigate. The water swirls into menacing whirlpools and eddies and hides many dangerous shoals. Only skilled captains may navigate ships through the most treacherous part of the St. Lawrence River."

Just then, a huge freighter passed them from the opposite direction. Colleen gasped at its size, her heart pumping alarm. Seeing the ships from the safe distance of the island's shore was one thing. Experiencing its massive power just feet from their steamer was quite another. Tara squeezed her arm tighter. Her eyes were wide with fear.

Jack eased their fears. "Captain Comstock is a skilled and savvy navigator. Relax, ladies, and enjoy the ride."

Colleen released her fear and allowed the magnificence of the St. Lawrence River to fill her mind's eye. She purposefully branded it all into her memory to sketch and paint in the days to come.

She would savor every moment of its allure.

And later, she'd paint the scars.

~ ~ ~

Jack sauntered next to Colleen, the sandy beach squishing under his feet, long shadows of the evening playing with the light. His palms sweat and his heart raced, but he pasted on an air of nonchalance, even as he felt like he would explode at any moment.

He swallowed the lump that kept growing bigger and bigger with each minute he put off sharing his heart. "It's been quite a summer. War. Marshall. You."

Colleen chuckled, her creamy chocolate eyes teasing. "I hope you don't always lump me in with war and ogres."

Jack shook his head, plunging his hands in his pockets to steady them. "Never. But I'm still in awe of what you shared about ridding yourself of the tyrants and conflicts in your heart. I'm humbled and honored to know you, Colleen. Truly."

Colleen shrugged, clicking her tongue. "I'm a work in progress, a mere sketch of what, I think, God might have me become someday. But today was a big step toward that."

Jack admitted, "I guess we are all works in progress—at least until we get to heaven."

The humid, hazy evening mirrored his emotions. Sticky. Foggy. How could he tell her his news and say what needed to be said? Words failed him at times like these. He silently offered a prayer for help.

Colleen bent down, picked up a small stone, and tossed it in the water. Not with the force he'd seen her use before, but her face held a hint of melancholy, nonetheless. "We leave in two days." She turned to him. "I'll miss the island. I'll miss you, Jack."

He sighed a prayer for help. "I have news, Colleen."

Instantly, Colleen's eyes flooded with the sadness he'd seen so many times before. She bit her bottom lip, her brows pulling together in anguish. "Your family?"

He offered a half smile, trying to steady his thoughts and find the words. "I received a letter from them just this afternoon. They are safe, thank God. They fled to Switzerland and are entreating me to stay in America. To remain safe and make a life here."

Colleen heaved a deep, ragged breath. "Thank God. Will they emigrate, too?"

He shrugged, then raised an eyebrow "Perhaps one day. They hope the conflict will be short-lived and plan to return to the farm—if it's still there when this war is over. If not…"

She slipped her arm in the crook of his elbow and hugged him. "I pray the farm is untouched, and the war is over soon and everyone stays safe."

247

Jack uncorked what he'd bottled up for weeks. What he wanted to share with her but kept inside while she healed from her injuries. When she didn't need to worry over him. When she needed peace. Rest. Healing.

"I almost left, Colleen. I planned to join the Canadian troops fighting with the Brits and packed my bags. I was going to leave the very day you were hurt. Your accident kept me here, kept me from making a foolish move."

Colleen glanced up at him with eyes filling with tears. A small moan escaped her lips. "Then I'm glad I was injured. Glad I kept you from going to war. I would've mourned your leaving. Into the danger. Truly."

Jack slipped her hand from his elbow and took it in his. "The beatitudes say that those who mourn are blessed, that they will be comforted. I've seen God comfort you, Colleen, and it has given me faith. Faith to believe what could be. Faith to imagine a future bright with hope."

Colleen's eyes still held that terrible sadness. Her lips quivered, and she sucked in the bottom one before plopping her head on his chest. Sounds of soft whimpers sped up his pulse and squeezed his heart. Was she trying to say goodbye?

"I have more news, Colleen."

Her head rose and her tear-streaked face implored him. "Are you leaving? Please say you won't."

"I won't." He licked his lips. "Frank, the butler, summoned me to his office today."

Confusion crossed her gaze as she searched his face. "You'll receive a good reference, yes?"

He affirmed her. His future depended on how she responded to his plans. Could he share them properly or would he bungle it? "Yes, but that's not what Frank wanted. He's retiring. He wants to train me to take his place. But I'm not sure I should accept."

Colleen blinked and pulled back from him. "That is quite an honor."

She turned her back and observed the river.

Was she disappointed with the news? Upset that Frank offered him a position in the Clarks' Chicago residence? In his uneasiness, had he spoken to her in German without realizing it?

The nervous twitch on his temple jumped to life, taunting him to speak. "I... I love you, Colleen. I want to share my life with you. To engulf your heart with love so deep, so true, that it heals the broken pieces of your life. I want to love you so fully that it sweeps away your pain forever."

Dummkopf.

With her back to him? That wasn't how he should declare his love.

Colleen's head snapped his way. "You what?"

"I love you."

Before he realized what was happening, Colleen fell into his arms and squeezed him tight. For several moments, she clung to him, and he to her. For several more moments, he worried about how she would respond to his next words.

But now, he had hope.

He released her and stroked the back of her scarred hand with his thumb, then kissed it as tenderly as a warm summer breeze. "Let's sit for a few minutes. Shall we?"

She consented, and he led her to a nearby mound of soft grass, the evening dusk alive with warblers dancing and singing in the misty twilight.

After Colleen settled her skirts around her, she straightened her back and lifted her chin. "I must know once and for all. Are you going to war? I cannot bear the thought of it, Jack."

He held back a chuckle. How easily things got mixed up. "No. Not if I can help it. Not for Canada or Austria or America."

She blew out a breath and beamed, her fondue eyes melting. Then she laid her head on his chest and whispered, "I love you, too."

Jack stroked her silky locks, holding her close. "I can offer you little, except a love so deep that I know we can overcome anything together. I want my life to intertwine with yours until I share the air you breathe and overcome every fear you face. And I want to spend my life empowering you to grow in your God-given talents so you can bless the world with it. I have no ring, but Colleen, will you entrust your heart and life to this simple man and become my wife?"

~ ~ ~

Colleen pressed her ear to Jack's chest, listening to his heart thump wildly. Had she really heard the words he spoke, or had she just imagined them?

She lifted her head and studied his handsome face, his dark features beseeching an answer. "You... you want to marry me?"

Jack bobbed his head, his dark curls bouncing. "Yes. Yes, I do."

Everything in her wanted to agree, but she had questions. "Can a maid and an under butler marry? Would the Clarks approve?" She bit her bottom lip, her pulse racing under her collar. "I could never allow you to endanger such a coveted position for me."

Jack chuckled, a twinkle in his eyes calming her, soothing her. "I asked Frank those very questions. He assured me that both answers are yes. He also offered us a small apartment over the garage. It's nothing fancy, he said, but it would do for a newlywed nest."

She gleamed, then touched his face, the dark stubble scratchy under her fingertips. So manly. So... Her heart leaped inside her. "I would love to be your wife."

He brightened and murmured, "Oh, thank you, Lord!"

Then he pulled her close. Dipped her off balance. Her head nestled in the crook of his arm.

Cradled in his love. Secure. Safe. Her face just inches from his. His eyes gentle but hungry. Tender but longing.

His musky scent swirling in the breeze, engulfing her. Her lips quivered, craving to taste his.

But still he waited.

He explored her face with his loving gaze as a gentle finger traced her jawline, running it over her lips until they tickled. He swept a stray curl from her forehead and tenderly kissed the spot.

A tiny moan escaped her lips, and he blinked. Then the island and everything around them vanished from sight. Time stopped.

Jack gave her an almost imperceptible smile and brushed his lips over hers. She licked hers, wanting them to stop quivering. But then he grinned and kissed her, this time in earnest, and her eyes fluttered shut.

She wanted to spread her wings and fly.

Soar on the wings of love.

Like the majestic eagle.

Free.

EPILOGUE

Two days later, Colleen stood on the back porch of Comfort Island cottage. Large, puffy clouds waltzed across the bright blue sky in the cool of the morning while she waited for the signal to descend the steps and start her new life.

Sunshine sparkled like diamonds on the river and peeped through the trees. The competing honks of the osprey, ducks, and geese calling to one another wafted on the wind. So did the delicious scent of pine.

They'd leave the island today, all of them, to winter in Chicago. And hopefully, they'd return to this beautiful piece of the world next year.

Colleen thanked God for the heaven-sent gift of this place. This new beginning of her life. And Jack. In mere minutes she would be his wife, and she'd launch into a future bright with hope.

She giggled with joy as she gazed at the bouquet of yellow lilies in her hands, tied with a white silk ribbon. Her creamy chiffon dress, a gift from Mrs. Lacey, had delicate, intricate tatting at the neck and sleeves and along the bell-shaped hem.

Just then, the majestic bald eagle swooped overhead as if to bless the day. She gave a little twirl, like a princess in a fairytale dream.

In the porch's eave, a late clutch of baby wrens chattered congratulations. Gulls squawked and soared as if they wanted to join the celebration. Champ scampered between the front porch and the back as if he was running the show.

Aunt Gertie stuck her head out the kitchen door and beamed, revealing several missing back teeth. Had Colleen ever seen her smile? Not until today.

"It's time."

Colleen consented as butterflies took flight in her stomach. She put a hand to her middle, took a deep breath, and swallowed her excitement, ready to face her new life.

~ ~ ~

Jack shifted from foot to foot, waiting for his bride to round the corner of the cottage and ascend the steps of the Comfort cottage veranda. The ten who waited for the ceremony to begin included Mrs. Clark, Mr. Alson and his wife, Frank, Tara, and Cook—Colleen's aunt—besides a few others. Reverend Wood came from the bay to make it official.

Champ climbed the steps and joined Jack, as if he were announcing the bride. He didn't bark, but he licked Jack's hand with his slobbery tongue.

When Jack whispered, "Sit, boy," the dog complied. Then he pulled out his handkerchief and wiped off his hand. A few titters of amusement trickled through the audience.

If only they could wed alone, just the two of them. In private. He wasn't one for public events.

But this was a special day, and those who attended were part of their story. A story of love, hope, and redemption.

And promise.

~ ~ ~

Following the ceremony, Colleen sat next to her husband at their delicious *el fresco* luncheon. Staff had pulled the long table from the dining porch onto the open veranda, just for them. Cook provided a feast of fried chicken, coleslaw, potato salad, and a pretty, buttercream frosted cake with raspberry jam in the middle. She had never tasted anything so heavenly.

Tara handed them each a cup of punch. "Wait until you taste this. It's lemonade with raspberries. Cook made it for your special day."

Colleen took the glass and smiled. "Thank you. All of you have made this so special."

Mr. Alson cleared his throat. "A toast to the bride and groom. May you embrace your individual stories but create a new one full of love and hope."

Everyone cheered and clinked their glasses, but he wasn't done. "And to that end, I offer you this as a wedding gift."

He slipped an envelope out of the inside of his coat and smiled at Jack, but handed it to Colleen. Strange that he'd give it to her and not defer to her husband.

She blinked back her surprise. "Thank you, sir."

Her hands trembled as she took the gift. She was about to hand it to Jack when Mr. Alson stopped her.

"You open it." His gaze was somber. Serious. "Now."

Were the Clarks dismissing her now that she was a married woman? What else could it be? In the past few days, they hadn't mentioned her future with them except to congratulate her marriage. Perhaps she was to be relegated to the two rooms above the garage. And they thought that a gift?

She studied Jack, who encouraged her to open it, a flicker of concern passing through his gaze. She turned it over and slipped a finger under the flap, and slowly removed the letter. When she opened it, a bewildering sigh escaped her lips. The sender addressed the missive to Mr. Alson Skinner Clark, not to her. Was the letter a mistake?

"Sir?"

Mr. Alson chuckled. "Read it."

She scanned the letter, and her heart thumped wildly. Her mouth went dry, so she licked her lips. Her knees trembled, but she shifted in her seat and straightened her spine.

It couldn't be. Could it?

Colleen snapped a glance at her husband and then smiled at Mr. Alson. She let out a little giggle and read.

Dear Sir,

Your prodigy, Miss Colleen Sullivan, shows great promise in the samples you submitted. Her compositions reflect emotional vulnerability, and a unique ethos energizes her work. The committee hereby offers her a position in the upcoming class at The Women's Art Institute of Chicago beginning September 15, 1914.

Sincerely,

Mrs. Josephine Merryweather

Jack threw back his head and laughed, his handsome face gleaming with joy. "Well, what do you know about that? My beautiful wife, the soon-to-be famous artist."

He kissed her on the mouth, in front of everyone. She swatted at him, her cheeks burning.

Mr. Alson shook Jack's hand. "Congratulation on a fine match. We will plan for her to stay in our employ as well as attend the institute, if that's agreeable with you."

Jack accepted. "Thank you, sir. Absolutely, if that works for you, wife."

Colleen laughed with abandon. "Yes! Yes. Thank you, both."

She dabbed happy tears with her handkerchief, her heart soaring on the breeze.

She no longer feared her story.

Instead.

She'd paint it.

~ ~ ~ THE END ~ ~ ~

ABOUT THE AUTHOR

Susan G Mathis is an international award-winning, multi-published author of stories set in the beautiful Thousand Islands, her childhood stomping ground in upstate NY. Susan has been published more than twenty times in full-length novels, novellas, and non-fiction books.

Her first two books of The Thousand Islands Gilded Age series, *Devyn's Dilemma,* and *Katelyn's Choice* have each won multiple awards, and book three, *Peyton's Promise*, comes out May 2022. *Colleen's Confession* is her newest title, and *Rachel's Reunion* is coming soon. *The Fabric of Hope: An Irish Family Legacy*, *Christmas Charity*, *Sara's Surprise,* and *Reagan's Reward* are also award winners. Susan's book awards include two Illumination Book Awards, three American Fiction Awards, two Indie Excellence Book Awards, and two Literary Titan Book Awards. *Reagan's Reward* is also a finalist in the Selah Awards.

Before Susan jumped into the fiction world, she served as the Founding Editor of *Thriving Family* magazine and the former Editor/Editorial Director of 12 Focus on the Family publications. Her first two published books were nonfiction, co-authored with her husband, Dale. *Countdown for Couples: Preparing for the Adventure of Marriage* with an Indonesian and Spanish version, and *The ReMarriage Adventure: Preparing for a Life of Love and Happiness*, have helped thousands of couples prepare for marriage.

Susan is also the author of two picture books, *Lexie's Adventure in Kenya* and *Princess Madison's Rainbow Adventure*. Moreover, she is published in various book compilations including five *Chicken Soup for the Soul* books, *Ready to Wed*, *Supporting Families Through Meaningful Ministry*, *The Christian Leadership Experience*, and *Spiritual Mentoring of Teens*. Susan has also several hundred magazine and newsletter articles.

Susan is vice president of Christian Authors Network (CAN) and a member of American Christian Fiction Writers (ACFW). For over twenty years, Susan has been a speaker at writers' conferences, teachers' conventions, writing groups, and other organizational gatherings.

Susan makes her home in Monument, CO, enjoys traveling globally, and relishes each time she gets to visit with her four granddaughters. Visit www.SusanGMathis.com for more.

BOOKS BY SUSAN G MATHIS
Visit: www.SusanGMathis.com/fiction

Peyton's Promise
Book 3 of the Thousand Islands Gilded Age series, coming May, 2022
Heritage Beacon Fiction (2022) 978-1645263449

Summer 1902. Peyton Quinn is tasked with preparing the grand Calumet Castle ballroom for a spectacular two-hundred-guest summer gala. As she works in a male-dominated position of upholsterer and fights for women's equality, she's persecuted for her unorthodox ways. But when her pyrotechnics-engineer-father is seriously hurt, she takes over the plans for the fireworks display despite being socially ostracized.

Patrick Taylor, Calumet's carpenter and Peyton's childhood chum, hopes to win her heart, but her unconventional undertakings cause a rift. Peyton has to ignore the prejudices and persevere, or she could lose her job, forfeit Patrick's love and respect, and forever become the talk of local gossips.

Devyn's Dilemma
Book 2 of the Thousand Islands Gilded Age series
Heritage Beacon Fiction (2020) ISBN-13: 978-1645262732

Devyn McKenna is forced to work in the Towers on Dark Island, one of the enchanting Thousand Islands. But when Devyn finds herself in service to the wealthy Frederick Bourne family, her life takes an unexpected turn.

Brice McBride is Mr. Bourne's valet as well as the occasional tour guide and under butler. Brice tries to help the mysterious Devyn find peace and love in her new world, but she can't seem to stay out of trouble—especially when she's accused of stealing Bourne's money for Vanderbilt's NYC subway expansion.

Katelyn's Choice
Book 1 of the Thousand Islands Gilded Age series
Heritage Beacon Fiction (2019) 978-1946016720

Katelyn Kavanagh's mother dreamed her daughter would one day escape the oppressive environment of their Upstate New York farm for service in the enchanting Thousand Islands, home to Gilded Age millionaires. But when her wish comes true, Katelyn finds herself in the service of none other than the famous George Pullman, and the transition proves anything but easy.

Thomas O'Neill, brother of her best friend, is all grown up and also working on Pullman Island. Despite Thomas' efforts to help the irresistible Katelyn adjust to the intricacies of her new world, she just can't seem to tame her gossiping tongue—even when the information she's privy to could endanger her job, the 1872 re-election of Pullman guest President Ulysses S. Grant, and the love of the man of her dreams.

~ ~ ~

Reagan's Reward
Thousand Islands Brides, book 3
smWordWorks (2020) 978-0692686645

Reagan Kennedy assumes the position of governess to the Bernheim family's twin nephews, and her life at Cherry Island's Casa Blanca becomes frustratingly complicated. Service to a Jewish family and tending to eight-year-old mischievous boys brings trouble galore.

Daniel Lovitz serves as the island's caretaker and boatman. When he tries to help the alluring Reagan make sense of her new world, her insecurities mount as her confidence is shaken—especially when she crosses the faith divide and when Etta Damsky makes her life miserable. As trouble brews, Daniel sees another side of the woman he's come to love.

Sara's Surprise
Thousand Islands Brides, book 2
smWordWorks (2019) 978-1087235714

Katelyn's best friend, Sara O'Neill, works as an assistant pastry chef at the magnificent Thousand Islands Crossmon Hotel where she meets precocious, seven-year-old Madison and her charming father and hotel manager, Sean Graham. But Jacque LaFleur, the pastry chef Sara works under, makes her dream job a nightmare.

Sean has trouble keeping Madison out of mischief and his mind off Sara. Though he finds Sara captivating, he's jealous of LaFleur and misreads Sara's desire to learn from the pastry chef as love. Can

Sean learn to trust her and can Sara trust him—and herself to be an instant mother?

Christmas Charity
Thousand Islands Brides, book 1
smWordWorks (2017) 978-0578207797

Susan Hawkins and Patrick O'Neill find that an arranged marriage is much harder than they think, especially when they emigrate from Wolfe Island, Canada, to Cape Vincent, New York, in 1864, just a week after they marry—with Patrick's nine-year-old daughter, Lizzy, in tow. Can twenty-three-year-old Susan Hawkins learn to love her forty-nine-year-old husband and find charity for her angry stepdaughter? With Christmas coming, she hopes so.

The Fabric of Hope: An Irish Family Legacy
smWordWorks (2017) 978-1542890861

An 1850s Irish immigrant and a 21st-century single mother are connected by faith, family, and a quilt. Will they both find hope for the future? After struggling to accept the changes forced upon her, Margaret Hawkins and her family take a perilous journey on an 1851 immigrant ship to the New World, bringing with her an Irish family quilt she is making. A hundred and sixty years later, her great granddaughter, Maggie, searches for the family quilt after her ex-pawns it. But on their way to creating a family legacy, will these women find peace with the past and embrace hope for the future, or will they be imprisoned by fear and faithlessness?

Other books by Susan G Mathis

Countdown for Couples: Preparing for the Adventure of Marriage

The ReMarriage Adventure: Preparing for a Lifetime of Love & Happiness

Lexie's Adventure in Kenya, a children's picture book

Princess Madison's Rainbow Adventure, a children's picture book

Susan is also an author in various book compilations including five *Chicken Soup for the Soul* books,

269

Ready to Wed, Supporting Families Through Meaningful Ministry, and several more.

Visit her at www.SusanGMathis.com
sign up for her newsletter
and please consider writing an Amazon review.
Thanks!